ISLAND

ISLAND

Patrick Downes

Groundwood Books
House of Anansi Press
Toronto / Berkeley

Groundwood Books / House of Anansi Press
groundwoodbooks.com

We gratefully acknowledge the Government of Canada for its financial
support of our publishing program.

With the participation of the Government of Canada | Canadä
Avec la participation du gouvernement du Canada

Library and Archives Canada Cataloguing in Publication
Downes, Patrick, author
Island / Patrick Downes.

Issued also in electronic formats.
ISBN 978-1-77306-192-4 (hardcover).—ISBN 978-1-77306-193-1
(EPUB).—ISBN 978-1-77306-194-8 (Kindle)

I. Title.

PZ7.1.D69Isl 2019   j813'.6   C2018-903526-9
                                            C2018-903527-7
Jacket illustration and design by Michael Solomon

Groundwood Books is committed to protecting our natural environment.
As part of our efforts, the interior of this book is printed on paper that
contains 100% post-consumer recycled fibers, is acid-free and is processed
chlorine-free.

Printed and bound in Canada

MIX
Paper from
responsible sources
FSC
www.fsc.org   FSC® C016245

ISLAND

ONE

I don't hear anyone fall. I don't hear a body crash down through the trees or break on the rocks. I don't hear anyone let out a last sigh.

Key —

My brother. I feel his terror.

Key's mind doesn't speak to my mind the way people imagine between twins. No brotherly pleading inside my own head. No *Rad, come — come now.* Not exactly.

I'm walking home, down below the house, the path along the ravine, and I lose my balance. Ground and sky switch places, and I want to throw up.

I pull my earbuds out of my head, lean against a tree, and retch.

Key?

I hear nothing. I look up through the woods toward the wall of the ravine. No window through the trees, no way to see my brother, but that doesn't matter. I know where he is, my twin, hidden from everyone but me by trees and ridges of rock.

I'm coming.

Twelve minutes around the end of the ravine, up two long, steep streets and the short dogleg that leads to our dead end.

We live on a cul-de-sac. The blacktop comes right to our ragged yard — no curb, no sidewalk — right to our crumbling driveway with purple-flowered weeds and dandelions and grass growing through the tar. A twenty-year-old Subaru wagon stands in the driveway with its bald tires and fringes of rust, keys in the ignition, waiting like an ancient, reliable horse.

Nine paving stones that resemble broken teeth lead from the street to our front steps.

Up one, up two.

Key? I shout it, or I might not say it at all. I don't know. Sometimes the words I think to say don't get past my lips.

"Key —?" Aloud this time. "You here?"

We live on a slant. You enter the house on level ground. Then, just inside the door, you feel an invisible hand tug you downhill toward the back of the house. If you set a marble on the floor of the vestibule and wait a few seconds, whisper your name or count to five, the pull of gravity will start the marble rolling. The marble will roll through the entryway and on between the lifeless living room and the staircase to the second floor. It'll pick up speed through the dining room where my family has laughed and bled. It'll hum right on through the doorway to the kitchen my father once destroyed in a rage and cruise past the basement door, the cupboards, to a lip of wall at the back door. That marble will jump the threshold out onto the deck and run the channel between two gray and splintered boards until it drops off the end.

As soon as I'm in the house, I feel that tug, gravity pulling me toward the back door. I go through the house.

No Key.

He must be outside.

I go downstairs and walk out of the basement onto the gravel and dirt and weeds under the deck. Blades of sunlight guillotine down between the boards.

I stop before the ladder of wood slats and steel cord my father fastened into the ledge at the top of the ravine. My father's ladder into the abyss. This is land's end. Another step, and I risk tumbling on down through the brush and bramble and thorns and stones and the trees growing out of the steep wall that ends at the bottom of the ravine.

The ladder disappears over the edge of the ravine. It dangles a few feet over a platform my father secured to the stone, a platform where he likes to sit alone on a rickety folding chair that leans left. Key and I have imagined, maybe daydreamed, my father falling asleep on that weak chair and sliding off before catching himself. He sits on his chair and looks out past the ravine toward the other side, toward the path where passersby walk or run, sometimes with their dogs. My father sits by himself in the quiet of the trees and vines and raw stone.

I am standing above the ladder.

And my brother? He must be down on the platform.

Why, Key?

I drop to my hands and knees. My brother and I have never gone down to the platform. But I can see my brother, alone, from the top of the ladder, and I descend, slat by slat by slat.

"Key?"

My brother, rocking back and forth on his heels, his hands over his ears as if to shield himself against a terrible noise.

"What's happening?"

Nothing so loud. Maybe the trees creaking in the wind, the warming world opening up to spring.

Murmuring. Maybe Key is murmuring.

"Key?"

My brother, useless, rocking, and I feel sick.

Look, something whispers without whispering, directly into my ear. *Just look.*

I stoop, kind of bend my knees and shuffle to the end of the platform. That strange sensation fills my legs, that sensation that makes you think you'll jump from where you're standing, the sensation that makes you think you'll throw yourself to your death.

Do you see?

I'm not sure what I think at first, what first comes to mind. Maybe a word: *Blood* or *Muscle* or *Bone.* Maybe *Help.*

To be honest, I think the very first thing that strikes me is the impossible angle of the body's left leg. I can't swear to it. If you've ever seen something so terrible that your mind has a hard time understanding your eyes, then you know you can't remember anything about the order of thoughts. Really, in that moment, you want to stare. You want to take all the time in the world to understand, to get it through your head what you're actually looking at. You might want to get closer.

There's no way I can get closer to the body even if I want to. Not without falling through the trees and onto the rocks.

I stand on the platform for a minute that feels like an hour, trying to understand the scene. The body of a man, my father, his twisted, shattered leg, his blood and bone. My father, whose face I can't make out, broken and dead on a ledge of rock thirty feet below, still far above the bottom of the ravine.

No sound. No sound.

■

For a long time, or what feels like a long time, Key and I say nothing at all. The first voice I hear is my own.

"We have to go," I say. "Now."

My brother, shaking his head, slapping at his ears as if a bug has crawled into his head.

I kneel down next to him. "Look at me, Key. We have to get away from here."

Key tries to speak, but it comes out all wrong, more like a choking.

He tries again.

"I don't know what happened."

"That doesn't matter right now."

"I don't know what happened."

"You have to get up." I reach down to help my brother to his feet, but he falls back.

"We were talking here, Rad. Then —."

I hold my hand out. "Come on, Key. You don't have to know anything yet."

Key lets me pull him to his feet. We make our slow way up the dangerous ladder, forty slats toward the rough, climbing ground, toward the loose stones and scraggly land and the shadow of the back porch, up and up toward our rotting house.

■

We barely take a few steps beyond the ladder before my brother collapses and falls over onto his side, as if his heart has stopped or he's been hit with a hammer.

"No." Here, the land can give out. Someone can fall. "Not here."

I shout my brother's name. Nothing.

I shake him.

"Key."

Nothing.

I hook my hands under Key's shoulders and haul him up onto his feet. Dead weight, and I nearly fall over backward. I take a step to catch myself.

We might die if my foot slips or misses the ground entirely, sending the two of us into the ravine.

Fear makes me angry.

"Key." I grind out his name through my teeth. I push back against his weight.

Have you ever wrestled a person who has given up? Wrestled with a 150-pound sack of wet muscle and hard bone? Even with someone much lighter, it's nearly impossible to get in control.

Helplessness makes me angry.

I take a deep breath and shove my brother, drive him toward the porch until we fall in a heap.

"Everything is jagged." Key, finally, and he wrenches himself out from under me. "The blood. I don't know what's happening."

Key, on his knees, heaving, and his pain, his loss of control, makes me angry.

I have my rage. My rage burns me up from the inside, hotter than a star, endless.

In my rage, I lift Key off the ground in a clumsy hug.

"You're my brother," I growl. "I've got you."

■

Key and I are fraternal twins, alike but not identical. I'm older by three minutes, taller by three inches, and I run three hundred times hotter. My emotions, what my mother called my weather, raw and uncontrollable.

I am, my father used to say, changeable. Key, with his immense vocabulary, calls me quixotic. One moment I'm all sunlight, rational, logical, calm. And the next I'm in full storm, irrational, illogical, wild, and serious as murder. I am impossible to predict. Any order to the chaos comes and goes. I can go from laughing to crying, crying to laughing without know- ing why. But what everybody fears is my instant rage. And by everybody, I mean everybody, especially me.

I am like the weather on Saturn. On Saturn, lightning can measure ten thousand times hotter than lightning on earth.

But Key, my twin, he's a different story. Even- keeled and easy-going, my brother, kind and infinitely gentle. Meditative and airy.

He also might have killed our father.

I wrestle Key through our basement door and stretch him out on the sunken corduroy couch. The damp, cool basement smells of mold and laundry and shadows. But it has a strange, calming effect. It's in a kind of twilight, not light, not dark. I come here when I feel upset. I pore over my pocket atlas and lose myself.

I lay out my brother. He sleeps or lies there unconscious while I sit on the floor with my back against the couch, waiting for him to wake up.

You wonder why I don't call an ambulance or the police, or why I don't go back down the ladder to look at my father on the rocks. I don't want to do anything at all until Key and I talk. So I sit, and I wait, and I drift off into sleep, or a waking dream, maybe into my brother's dream. Who knows?

Key and I sit at the center of a maze. White halls like hospital halls leading every which way disappear into points of light. Infinite hallways open in every direction. One of the hallways has a blue stripe painted down its center.

Key says, "Let's get out of here."

"The blue line?"

"What else?" And my brother starts down the bright white corridor with the blue stripe that might go on for a thousand miles.

"Rad?"

"Hm?"

"Rad, I'm here."

"I know."

"I mean, wake up. I'm here."

I come to and take in my brother, exhausted but upright, standing over me.

"I just had a dream," I say.

"I could tell."

I nod and push myself up onto my feet. "Let's go up to the kitchen."

All around us a crowd of ghosts, multiples of one ghost, my father.

"That's pretty quick."

Key on the stairs ahead of me, walking among the ghosts. "What are you talking about?"

"The ghosts, Key. All the ghosts. Dad in ectoplasm."

"Rad, it's time to wake up."

"Yeah, right."

The kitchen feels empty and lonely and entirely full. A hundred ghosts of my father wall to wall, covering the ceiling, sitting in the sinks, on top of the refrigerator, everywhere, silent and indifferent, standing, sitting, stretching, watching.

I remember the day my mother died, eight years ago when Key and I were nine, and her ghosts, all her ghosts. My mother repeated and repeated, filling the house, standing and sitting on top of each other, no room.

"You want some water?" I pour two glasses from a pitcher of tap water we keep in the refrigerator and hand one to my brother. The ghosts seem uninterested.

Key nods.

"Aren't you going to ask, Rad?"

I drink through one glass of water and pour another. "What do you mean?"

My brother shakes his head. "Why are you playing stupid? I killed him. I killed Dad."

I drink half my second glass of water. I'm so thirsty.

"Did you hear me?"

"I heard you, Key. What do you mean? You pushed him?"

My brother shakes his head. "I don't know," he says. "I might have."

And I can't help myself. I laugh. The laugh comes from someplace broken. And it disappears the moment it arrives, with the memory of my father's body.

"That seems like something you would either know or not know."

"I don't know anything." Key swallows down half his water, and I top up his glass. "Maybe I pushed him. Maybe I didn't, but how else could he —"

"No." I shake my head. "No. Uh-uh." I can't stop shaking my head. "No matter what, you did not kill Dad."

"Maybe I did."

"No, you didn't. You will not tell me you killed Dad. And you will not tell anyone else you killed Dad. Not the police, not anyone."

"I —" Key frowns. "Rad, our world has changed."

"You think?" Our father, dead in the ravine. My weather and storms coming closer. "What happened, Key?"

"Our world has changed."

"I don't understand."

"Maybe this will throw me over the edge."

"That's funny."

"What is?"

"Throw *you* over the edge?"

My brother looks like he might throw up.

"Key, please. You're the reasonable one, the one with a steady mind, and I'm the one —"

My brother sits in front of me, shaking all over, his hands in his lap.

I feel helpless.

"Key. Please. Talk."

My father broken and bloody. His ghosts crowding around us. My brother out of control, silent.

It's all too much.

So what do I do? I throw the water pitcher against the refrigerator. Totally unreasonable, totally irrational and stupid. Totally me.

I stand up fast, toppling my chair, and throw the pitcher. When the pitcher smashes — the glass and water — Key jumps. A shocked second.

And I reach for my glass to throw that, too.

"Rad." Key covers the glass with his hand. "This is not the time."

I yank the glass out from under his hand.

My brother, his giant green eyes, the green eyes I have, my brother, reaching out to me.

"Put the glass down, Konrad."

He uses my name.

I put the glass down, even more upset for my embarrassment, for upsetting Key, and go for dish towels in the drawer next to the sink. The sea of ghosts parts for me.

"I killed —"

"You did not kill anyone," I shout. I stare down at the shattered pitcher, the glass and water all over the floor, and my emotion drains out of me, adding to the mess. Out of nowhere, as fast as my rage, my calm.

I pick up my chair.

"I'm not angry at you, Key."

When I'm unable to do anything for my brother, when I'm unable to do anything to help myself or my father or anybody —

It's the helplessness that makes me crazy. But my sudden rages only make matters worse. I never learn.

"I never learn," I say from my hands and knees, the garbage pail next to me. I start to pick up shards of glass. The way the pitcher broke, one side remained intact, and a little pool of water shivers in its shallow bowl. "I'm sorry, Key."

The broken glass, the water, and I have already sliced two fingers.

"The trouble's only starting, Rad."

"I know." The glass in the pail and my bloody fingers. "How did Dad fall, Key? What happened down there?"

TWO

I love maps. And I especially love islands. We once had a *National Geographic* atlas from the 1990s. I studied it whenever I could, until I threw it off the back porch during a fit. I threw the atlas down into the ravine, lost forever, but I bought myself another old atlas, one I use almost every day.

I have a goal to memorize the world's known islands, or at least the ones that show up on common maps and have names. It's an impossible goal. There are more islands on the planet than we can identify even with satellites, easily more than a hundred thousand. In my whole life, I've memorized about fifteen hundred — 1,487, to be exact. Not quite the number of islands just in the Florida Keys. That's 1,487 islands organized by regions and bodies of water. I use the goal to calm myself down when I feel like I'm losing control. If I feel the wildness, my emotions rising inside of me, flooding me, I go to the atlas, to the world's islands and archipelagos. I even carry a pocket atlas, a gift to myself. I carry it in my backpack, always. When I feel overwhelmed, I set myself adrift in two-dimensional oceans and seas and lakes. I find islands. And then I get lost in jungles, forests, mountains, lava, and ice.

When I'm upset, I throw myself into paper oceans. I calm myself through land and water I've never seen. And it works — most of the time. Sometimes nothing helps, not even a map of the world. I once tossed the whole world away, even if the world was made only of maps, of paper, ink, and glue. Embarrassing. Sometimes my emotions threaten to swallow the universe. But a lot of the time I can calm down a little in the atlas, in the names of islands.

I've studied the names of the islands in the Kodiak and Sulu archipelagos; the names of the Queen Elizabeth Islands, the Isles of Scilly, the Bajuni and Sa'ad ad-Din, the Madeleines and the Turku, the Cyclades, the Orkneys, and the Islands of the Four Mountains. Islands from cold (the Balleny) to warm (the Riau), tiny (Bishop Rock) to enormous (Greenland), close (Nantucket or Bainbridge) to remote (Bouvet). Island prisons (Robben and Devil's) to islands for outlaws (New Providence). I study the names of contested islands, like the Kurils, not too far north of Hokkaido, also an island, Japan's northernmost, one famous for volcanoes and ski resorts. The fight for sovereignty over the Kuril Islands has kept Russia and Japan from signing a peace treaty to end World War II.

Islands.

To me, Earth is an island. We're surrounded on all sides by an ocean of space and no other habitable planets. Or none that we know of. Yet.

I'd like to live on an island. An island I can walk end to end, or the full circumference, in less than a day. I want to know I'm surrounded by water. I can't swim, so I would be stranded until I find a boat or until the water freezes or someone builds a bridge, or I perform a miracle. Otherwise I'll die at the edge of the ocean. I want to live on an island off the coast of Maine, maybe, or one of the two tiny sovereign French islands between Newfoundland and Cape Breton, or in Malaysia. I don't know.

It's easy to think people are islands. Too easy. Too easy to think I'm an island, my brother and, before they died, my mother and my father. Everyone. It's too easy, especially when we're sad or angry. But some have argued we can't ever really connect with anyone else. They say we stand alone, always, forever. And maybe that's true.

Or do we always have one connection somewhere, a thread, weak and thin but still real?

Except we want to be unique and pretend we're isolated right up until it gets scary, until it gets lonely.

And then there's the other side. None of us is ever truly alone and apart. "No man is an island," blah, blah. So cliché, right? Though not when John Donne wrote it almost four hundred years ago. A lot of very smart people have decided it's true, that we're all connected. "A piece of the continent," like Donne says, "part of the main." Yeah, we want to feel attached at least to one other person, or to the spirit of the world.

Until we don't.

Until we think we're bored, until we want to pretend we're alone, unique. It's like everything else with us, with people. Our minds play tricks on us. Sometimes we feel connected, want to feel connected, and sometimes we don't, or don't want to. We can never really be sure of anything. We always make trouble for ourselves. It's no wonder we're not happy for very long.

But what if we have no brothers or sisters or parents or grandparents or friends or enemies or guardians or anyone, anyone at all, to run into over and over again? If we have no obvious connections? Then do we become islands? Or do we always have one connection somewhere, a thread, weak and thin but still real, a connection?

I don't know if people are or aren't islands. Maybe we are and aren't at the same time.

Families are islands for sure. Even families living in an archipelago, on a city street, in a housing project or a planned community, living close enough to shout to each other. They're still surrounded on all sides by water. They still have their own land and climate and geography. They are unique.

A family is a strange landscape, isolated. And we can always find wilderness.

∎

I read a long novel for an independent study in eleventh-grade English. Leo Tolstoy's *Anna Karenina*. Honestly, I picked it based on the first sentence, which I found online occupying sixth place on a list of 100 Best First Lines of Novels. I also considered *Scaramouche* ("He was born with a gift for laughter and a sense that the world was mad," #99) and *The Color Purple* ("You better not never tell nobody but God," which takes a little working out, at #37).

Forget about the rest of *Anna K.* I could have written the required 3,500-word essay about Tolstoy's first sentence:

"All happy families are alike; each unhappy family is unhappy in its own way."

True? Not true? Tolstoy must have thought people would think it over, argue it. It's one of those ideas with a trapdoor.

Each unhappy family ... each unhappy family ...

The sentence echoed inside of me. My family's life was nothing like the unhappy lives in Tolstoy's book, with their unfaithful, jealous, greedy lives and whatever else. But that's Tolstoy's point, I guess. My family's unhappiness is different from the unhappiness of the Karenins and the Oblonskys and the Levins of the novel, but we're all unhappy, fictional or not, each in our way.

It's hard to stay happy for very long. Even when we're alone, sitting by ourselves without anyone else around to mess things up, our happiness can't last. Minding our business on our own little island, anything can go sideways at any time. We can get sick.

We can get bored. We can get lonely. We can hate ourselves.

Happiness is always at risk.

We can do our best: study, sleep eight to ten hours a night, stay away from drugs and alcohol and dangerous sex and screens and phones and apps and Netflix. We can eat less sugar, less salt, or more sugar and more salt. Drink less Coke, drink more Coke. We can exercise. We can volunteer, or work, like Key and I do, for an actual paycheck to put toward food and bills and college and clothes, or to help house and family.

Family. Other people.

We can't avoid thinking about other people no matter how much we might try to think only about ourselves. We can be fair. We can never say anything mean or cruel. We can steal from the rich and give to the poor. We can stick up for others or fight for a better world, protest, sign petitions, whatever. We can love.

We can do all these things to be good. But still we can be unhappy. We can be hurt. We can lie. We can scream and yell. We can be betrayed. We can betray.

Our happiness can last only as long as we can avoid screwing something up or escape everything in the world that can hurt us, including ourselves. We're imperfect no matter what, always imperfect.

And if it's hard to be happy by ourselves, then it's got to be harder to be happy with someone else, even with someone you love. If I want to see any horror movie, no matter how bad, over any drama, no matter how good, but someone else, someone I love, like my suddenly ex-girlfriend, Jacqui, who would always take a drama over horror, then —

I'm sorry. I'm not really sure how Jacqui popped into my head there.

It's maybe even a simple, probably stupid example anyway.

"All happy families are alike; each unhappy family is unhappy in its own way."

There's only one way to be happy and an infinite number of ways to be unhappy. To be happy, everything has to go right. But to be unhappy, just one thing has to go wrong.

■

I figure most families are happy and unhappy at the same time. Sometimes they lean more toward happiness than unhappiness, or the other way around. They can go on like that, constantly tilting one way or another. This is the truth of family.

We see happy families and unhappy families, though, and we know the difference.

A happy family eats a breakfast of scrambled eggs and toast for dinner. A happy family sings around a piano. Or maybe a happy family picks up trash from the sidewalks and gutters on weekend mornings. One happy family camps together in a remote forest in Labrador every June, and another has two hundred cousins and aunts and nieces and nephews all sit down once a year to a reunion feast of boar and buffalo and ostrich, roasted corn and potato salad and egg salad, marshmallow ambrosia and chocolate-covered crickets. Maybe a happy family eats anchovy and onion pizzas on Fridays. Another pans for gold, and another takes turns reading aloud from the dictionary by candlelight. One binges on Hulu, and another prays ten times a day, and another keeps four dogs, six cats, a mute parrot, a giraffe, an iguana, and a two-headed goat.

All of this makes for a particular, sometimes strange happiness — not everyone prays, pans for gold, or keeps a menagerie — but we can't deny the happy family its happiness. That family, no matter what, feels safe with each other.

The unhappy family is made up of actors, sometimes really good liars who occasionally pretend happiness in public, like the cast of a sitcom who seem to love each other on camera but loathe each other when the camera is turned off. They can't eat a meal backstage together without an argument. We can't necessarily see where the danger or the unhappiness in a family comes from. It may be hidden from us, but that family knows the facts, even if they're not telling. We see the unhappy family, and nothing stops us from making up the story of its misfortune.

I don't want you making anything up about my family. I'll tell you what you want to know.

The family Key and I were born into included a man, my father, named John William Schoe (pronounced *shoo*), and a woman, my mother, Diane. My mother died when Key and I were nine.

She was walking to work early in the morning when a tire struck and killed her. The tire belonged to a dump truck. It came off as the truck barreled down the avenue. According to two witnesses, the tire traveled almost three hundred yards before it swerved toward my mother.

My mother died on the street just as the paramedics arrived. They found her already gone. Around 6:15 a.m.

After the tire struck my mother, it tore through a storefront and destroyed a deli, seriously injuring the owner who had just begun to unwrap his daily trays of cheese.

Before my mother's death, we were happy. Or I think we were. Unhappiness can ruin happiness so fully that you wonder if you were ever happy at all, even for a second.

∎

No. We were happy, the four of us. I can tell you about it. Won't take long.

We didn't have a menagerie or pan for gold. We didn't sing together or go camping, and we had no cousins or aunts or uncles, since my parents were the only children of only children. What we had was a family that had fun. And nothing says fun like a family of four trying to set world records that no one else on earth can prove or disprove.

Who will say the four of us did — or did not — over a long Thanksgiving weekend simultaneously juggle for a half-hour each day on the busiest downtown street corner? Key and I were seven years old when our father taught us to juggle. Key was a natural. Even now he'll keep up five balls, five kittens, five bricks, five anything. Me? I can get my three tennis balls up, and that's where it ends. But over that weekend, my mother, Key and I juggled three balls each, and my father four cleavers, all on the street in front of a curious public. I dropped a ball once, maybe twice. And once my father let the four cleavers clatter to the pavement when a buddy passing by (no longer a buddy) called out my father's name to distract him. Better to drop the cleavers than lose a digit or two, a tragedy that would come later with another stunt. Over the two days we made $450 from all kinds of people tossing bills and coins at our feet. Our parents gave my brother and me each a hundred to open savings accounts.

No one but us can say for sure that all four of us jumped on our parents' king-sized bed for thirteen minutes and fifty seconds without stopping. We would have gone longer — much, much longer — if I hadn't fallen off and broken my wrist or, really, if the bed hadn't broken, sending me to the floor. I'm actually surprised the bed lasted as long as it did. Four people jumping together? How stupid. Key and I were eight for that one.

Who can say we didn't walk a mile together in less than twenty minutes, backwards?

Only four people on the planet know how many ears of corn my family once ate in fifteen minutes. And only four people know how many pumpkin pies — my father eating two pieces for every one of Key's — we polished off between 2:00 and 4:00 the afternoon of one November 14.

There were more grand attempts at private greatness, and some spectacular failures. We once blew up a toilet and flooded our basement. We lost a rental car in an Arkansas lake. My mother all but lost her voice forever during a singing marathon. And my father lost a pinky toe and the tip of a second toe to frostbite. That was during what my father called the Idiotarod, our version of dogsledding across Alaska. Some events ended in tears.

My parents would save money for this or that idea and take their risks with vacation and sick days, ask for time here and there. They would pull Key and me from school if they had to, but mostly we played within the rules and law. My father joked that when Key and I turned eighteen we would go on a crime spree, robbing banks and knocking over convenience stores, but the family didn't last that long.

Not that we would have turned to crime.

I don't think.

My parents had fun with each other before they married, and it mattered to them to keep a sense of adventure and goofiness after they married and gave birth to twins. They could get testy over logistics, moody over money, grumpy over my father's insistence that we carry out every ridiculous idea no matter what. But I only ever saw them fight once. That story has to wait.

It's important to know that my brother and I trusted our parents through all of our escapades, even the ones that ended poorly. We were a happy family.

■

I'm not so much telling a story as taking you somewhere. I'm taking you to an island, and you'll either come the whole way or leave off somewhere and turn back. I want you to come with me, though. I want you to come along until we say goodbye. Then I'll go my way and you'll go yours. I'm building a bridge, a wild bridge with arms, and you're walking it with me. You'll cross the water by the same bridge back to your land, to the country you know better, to your home. You'll have traveled a little. It's good to get out.

The biggest problem I have, whether or not I'm telling a story or getting you across a strait of water to an island, is picking the straightest route. I leave things out, too. Like what happened on my way home after I felt my brother's fear. The morning I saw my father's broken body. It took me twelve minutes to get home from the path at the bottom of the ravine, but it should have taken less than seven. Where did those minutes go?

For a minute, maybe more, I forgot what I was supposed to be doing, forgot where I was headed as I watched two black dogs wrestle in the grass. Growling, snarling, snapping, scraping.

Then, two minutes or so went to a series of one-sided texts I sent to Jacqui.

Me: I don't think we said everything before. At least I didn't.

I waited.

Me: I'm heading home. Something's up with Key. But let's meet in a couple hours, please.

Waited. Waited.

Me: OK Jac. I get it. You're upset. I was wrong to get so angry. We should talk. I'll talk. I promise.

And there's the business with the flashing lights and the accident scene that may or may not have happened.

Near the dead end where we live, far down the road, I saw flashing lights. Fire trucks, police, ambulances, I'm guessing. I couldn't tell.

Maybe if my brother wasn't going through some sort of terrible crisis I could feel, maybe if I didn't get sick again and have to retch into the curb — *Key* — I might have walked to the lights.

But what could I have done?

Nothing.

And to be perfectly honest, there might not have been an accident, nothing terrible at all.

Now and then, ever since the morning my mother was killed in the street, I imagine the scene. I imagine it from the distance of one of the witnesses who watched a truck tire fly down the street and, as if it had a mind of its own, kill a woman walking to work. I imagine the trucks and lights, and I imagine the disaster. I imagine my mother broken and bruised, crushed and shocked.

It took me a moment to take in the far-off lights, get sick on the curb and recover.

Maybe another minute or more. And then, home.

■

I sit at the kitchen table across from Key, who stares into his glass of water. He's just told me he killed our father, and I've finished cleaning up the pitcher I threw against the refrigerator.

We are surrounded by ghosts.

"You'll die young," he says. "Your emotions, Rad. They'll shorten your life."

My brother has foretold my future, a future entirely different from his, and I don't know what to say.

"Your heart eats at your brain. Or the other way around. It'll take years from you."

"I guess we'll see."

"You'll have whole years swallowed up by anger.

You'll torture yourself, and you might torture everyone around you. But the anger —"

"Okay," I plead. "Okay, okay."

Will I someday drown in my emotions? Will an undertow drag me right down under a crazy sea of sadness and happiness and rage? Maybe.

"That was rough," Key whispers. "I —"

"Maybe you're right. But that's still a ways off."

Silence.

"Makes you wonder, though, how it is *I* didn't kill Dad."

"So you do think I killed Dad."

"No, Key. I'm not saying you killed him. I know you didn't. I'm only wondering how I didn't."

"I don't know," Key admits. "You might have two nights ago."

The night my father beat up Key. "You're right. What he did —"

"But I needed you," Key said. "And he needed you. Remember? So you let him go."

"Yes."

"You don't always have to follow your emotions to some terrible place."

I see the trap. If I'm at the mercy of my emotions, then I'll go wherever they lead me, and I don't ever have to take real responsibility for being a monster. If I'm not at the mercy of my emotions, then I can

exercise some control and one day become a reasonable, mature human being capable of having friends,
a girlfriend who lasts, a job and a family — and I
will have the responsibility of getting myself under
control.

The fact is sometimes one instinct outweighs another. The night my father attacked my brother, my
instinct to help Key finally outweighed my instinct to
kill my father. I felt no more in control of myself that
night than any other. My mind's an ocean.

"Key," I say, breaking the quiet, "we have to talk
about what happened in the ravine. Just us. Before we
talk to anyone else."

"Before the police," he says. "A delayed response."

"Believable," I say. "In our shock, we didn't call.
Or —"

"We can call after we discover what happened,
sometime in the future, an hour or two from now."

"Something like that."

Key shook his head. "It's a lie, Rad."

"I know. But what choice do we have?"

THREE

I was standing with Dad right up until he was gone.
I watched him, Rad. As he fell.
It all happened in silence. Even the trees, the branches
that broke, and his back and his head and his legs —
Not a sound.

When I got to the platform, he asked me, "Did you pass my wife on your way down?"

Mom, Rad. He asked if I passed Mom, as if he didn't know who I was. I know it's not strange anymore, but it still makes me shiver. I said no.

"You didn't see Diane?" Dad looked confused. "That's strange. She just left, and I could hear her on the ladder. I was counting her steps. Thirty, thirty-one, thirty-two, all the way up, and then you came. How could you miss her?"

"I don't know," I said. "I can't explain it."

"Hm," Dad said and searched my face.

"How is she?" I said.

"Diane? I can't say for sure. Too happy, maybe. Excited, but she wouldn't tell me why."

"Why do you think?"

"I can't guess," Dad said, "but I didn't have the heart to tell her she's dead."

I thought I might break apart right there.

"You thought I didn't remember my wife's dead?" He shook his head. "Diane's dead all right, eight years, but I couldn't tell her that."

Dad watched me for a couple of seconds. He said, "What brings you here?"

"You do. Do you know who I am?"

"I guess I should," he said.

"Would you like me to tell you who I am?"

"Yes, please."

"I'm Key."

Dad frowned, smiled, frowned, smiled.

"Diane's son," I said. "Your son."

"Ha!" he laughed. "Last time I saw you, you were a skinny kid, thirteen or fourteen, all eyes and lips and feet. Look at you now. Come here. Let me give you a hug."

He held me, Rad. When was the last time Dad hugged us for his sake or ours? And he held me too hard. Clinging for life, maybe. I don't know. Then he stepped back away from me, arm's length, to take me in, you know? I thought he'd go over the side right then. But I had him in my hands, and he had me in his. He wouldn't let go.

"I miss Diane," he said.

"I know," I said. "You loved each other."

"Never a truer word," he said. "Whether I die now or in forty years, I will always miss my wife's light." He frowned again. "What happened to your face? Who did that to you?"

"My brother, Konrad," I said. Sorry I blamed you.

"Oh?" Dad's eyes flickered, but he pushed some thought away, or his memory. "You boys should take it easy. You got the worst of it, I guess."

I couldn't tell him, Rad. I couldn't tell him what he'd done to me.

■

I don't know when I took Key's hand. It didn't seem strange. We used to hold hands to and from school until fourth grade, right up until I had my butt kicked for it by —

Doesn't matter who. I got beat up for holding my brother's hand.

And I'm holding Key's hand now at the kitchen table, our father lying dead behind our house, his body food for insects, birds, and mice.

I hold my brother's hand while he tells me about what happened on the platform. I let go so he can wipe his nose with his shirt. I have to wipe my own face, and I realize I'm wearing a T-shirt Key gave me on our last birthday: *World's Okayest Brother*.

"Key, I have to know. Why did you go down there in the first place, to the platform?"

Key snorts and wipes his nose with the back of his hand. "What do you mean?"

"We don't ever go down there. So?"

Key sits very still, and I let go of his hand.

"Key?"

"I saw him go down, Rad. I saw him take the ladder."

"And?"

"And I had a bad feeling."

"What kind of bad feeling?"

"I don't know. After the other night —"

"Did you want to talk to him about what happened?"

"There's no talking to Dad. And anyway, he didn't remember anything about it."

"He almost killed you, Key. How could he forget?"

"I don't know, Rad. I don't think he was pretending not to know."

"Did you go to confront him?"

"No. I don't know. I didn't trust what he would do. I thought he might jump or something."

"Or something?"

"You were there, Rad. He almost killed me. You said so yourself. Maybe he felt guilty."

"You just said he acted like nothing had happened. He said he missed Mom. Is that when he fell, Key? After he told you he missed Mom?"

Key shakes his head. "No."

"Maybe he jumped."

"No, Konrad." He raises his hands. "Let me think."

"Maybe he remembered and felt guilty and jumped. Maybe —"

"Rad. No." Key clenches his fists against his eyes. "No, he didn't jump."

"What then?"

"Something like a dream. And when I woke up, Dad was falling away."

"A dream? I don't understand." I watch my brother.

"No," Key says. "I don't either."

■

I wasn't exactly honest when I said we were happy right up until my mother died. That would have been easier, I think. If we went instantly from happy to unhappy. But the true story is a little more complicated. It always is.

Seven months before my mother died, everything in our family changed. Key and I don't quite remember the moment the same way, but we agree deep trouble started the night my father asked for a drink.

My father, a lawyer then, got home from work one night a little on the early side, six or so, and emptied his pockets as he always did — his keys, wallet, pen knife, and change — onto the dining table. He left these things on the table with three gift-wrapped packages.

"Where is everybody?"

My mother was fixing dinner, and Key and I were playing in the basement. By the time Key and I got upstairs, our parents were kissing, and we greeted our father. We saw the gifts, and my father put his finger over his mouth to keep my brother and me quiet.

"I have news and I have gifts," our father said. "Which do you want first?"

"The news," Key said.

"All right, the gifts," my father said, and he winked at Key. Everything up to now felt right. My father in good humor, teasing Key and me, and my mother right there, close.

Then the train came off the tracks.

"Diane," my father said. "Pour me a drink."

My mother hesitated. "Sure," she said, a little slow. "Water?"

"No, Diane, an actual drink. Don't we have scotch?"

Key and I would count three things wrong with this exchange. First, my father only ever used my mother's name when he was stressed, or to call to her from another part of the house, or when he was around acquaintances, people we didn't really know well. Otherwise, our father called my mother by pet names. That night, before he asked for his drink, my father didn't seem anxious, my mother was standing right in front of him, and he had his family around, no friends, strangers, or acquaintances.

Second, my father only drank alcohol to pour a sip from a bottle of wine he'd bought my mother, to test it. Every so often a beer, but he never looked as if he enjoyed it.

Third, my father didn't sound like my father. He always had a low voice, and he tended to speak slow, almost with a drawl. But there he was, growling and biting off his words. The request, the order for a drink, which came without his usual politeness, without his *please* and *thank you*. It sounded threatening. As in, "Pour me a drink, Diane, or you'll be sorry."

Key and I glanced at each other and at our father.

He handed me a gift without looking at me. "We have scotch, yes?"

"Yes," my mother said. "Absolutely. One scotch coming up."

"Rad," my father said, "you're dawdling. Open it up."

It was a model I would have to put together. An airplane. Plastic. Whatever.

"Like it, buddy?" The word *buddy* sounded all wrong, as if he actually said *twerp*.

"Yes —"

"My drink," he interrupted. I knew right then, my father had already been drinking, might already be drunk, and I was scared. "Leave the bottle right there, Diane."

He handed Key his gift, my mother hers. "Which of my two lovelies should go first?" he said and drank back the scotch.

"I'll wait for Mom," Key said.

"No, darling," Mom answered, "you first."

"Well, one of you, please," my father spat. "Key, here, I'll help you." He took the gift out of my brother's hands and opened it up.

A brunette Barbie, for my brother who already —

"Take it," my father handed over the doll. "It's your last one for a long, long time."

Key smoothed the doll's hair and looked at Mom, who was staring at my father as he poured himself another drink.

My fear grew and grew, and I thought I might be sick. This man wasn't my father.

"John," my mother said. She only used his first name when she was nervous or needed him to focus. "What's happening?"

"We're sitting here, and my family's opening gifts. That's what's happening." He drank. "Your turn."

"John, this isn't right."

It seemed to take my father a minute or more to put down his empty glass and stand up. He seemed to be gathering all his strength. He held out my mother's gift. "Open it, Diane."

It sounded like, "Open it, Diane, or I'll kill you right here where you stand, in front of the children."

What with my father who was not my father, his voice not his voice; with my frightened mother, my mystified brother; with all the quiet and slowness and promise of violence; with the gifts that felt heavy as lead; with all my fear and helplessness —

I wet myself.

■

I've told you about my emotions. I got worse after my mother died. Much worse, no surprise. But when I was very young, I used to shake, throw tantrums, cry, and laugh and laugh until I'd pass out. Seriously, I'd lose consciousness laughing. And I'd wet myself.

I don't wet myself at all anymore. That's a good thing. I peed myself just once after that time in front of my mother and brother and the man I had known until then as my father, the man who would become a grief-stricken derelict. But that last accident was only a few years ago, when I was fourteen. It had nothing to do with fear or rage or laughing. I had forgotten to go to the bathroom before bed, and I dreamed of a very long and very satisfying pee, only to wake up having actually peed. I am being honest about this because I think everyone, or nearly everyone, has peed when they would rather have not peed, when they didn't expect they would pee, as in their sleep, or when they laughed, or when they were afraid or in pain. And I don't think I will ever wake from a pee dream without panicking. Honestly, I don't understand why we *wouldn't* pee during a vivid pee dream.

So, I have to correct myself. I haven't peed myself for years, but I might pee myself sometime in the future if I feel hurt, frightened, sick, or have an especially lifelike pee dream.

The last time I wet myself in company, though, I was eight. It happened that night my father asked for a drink, the same night, he later told my mother, he got into a fist fight with a client and then punched his partner, threw a printer against a wall, quit his job, and decided to withdraw from the life he had made with my mother.

The only dispute about that event is what happened after I wet myself.

I claim my father covered his face and sat down, and that my mother hurried me and my brother to the bathroom, got me into the tub, and found me fresh clothes. I don't know why my father covered his face, what he wanted to hide.

Key claims my father covered his face to hide his crying, and then my mother hurried me, and so on.

"You always think he covered his face because he was angry," Key says, when we get into it, which might even have been as recently as a month ago. "You don't remember Dad crying because you were embarrassed and afraid and couldn't see straight."

My brother's right, of course, about what I was feeling. But I don't remember my father crying. Not then, not ever. He didn't cry when the police came to let us know my mother had been killed. He didn't cry when we buried her. He didn't cry with Key and me when the love of his life, and our mother, evaporated. He didn't cry until —

To my brother, our father's crying matters.

"He was sad," Key argues. "And something in him had died."

"That's no excuse for anything at all."

This is the argument between Key and me. But what about my mother? Maybe the crying, if my father did cry, forced my mother to hold on after my father gave up. Maybe she would have held on all the way until now, never divorcing him, never pushing him out, taking care of him forever. My mother, like Key, might have thought the crying meant my father still had a heart, even if it was broken for reasons none of us knew. And as long as he had a heart, she would stick with him.

I don't know.

I peed myself and, according to Key, my father fell back into his chair crying and covered his face. A little while later, as my mother was washing down my legs in the tub, and my brother was sitting on the closed toilet examining the toilet paper, the wallpaper, the back of his hand, anything but his half-naked and humiliated brother, I said to my mother, "What did Dad give you?"

"I don't know," she said. "I didn't open it."

"Jewelry," Key said.

"A diamond necklace," I said.

My brother unwrapped that gift five years later when my father finally ran out of money. A bracelet of pearls Key sold to pay for electricity, or our gas bill, or for my glasses, or for food, or for water.

But I'm getting ahead of myself.

■

I'm leading you to an island, our island, across a bridge I'm constructing as we go.

My father and my mother loved each other. We were happy, happy in our silliness, and then we became unhappy.

When my mother, Key, and I went back out to the dining room, my father was gone.

"Just stay here," our mother said. "The two of you. Go upstairs to your rooms and wait."

Key and I watched our mother leave, and then we followed.

My mother found our father sitting behind the wheel of his car, his forehead on the steering wheel, keys in the ignition.

"John?"

No answer.

"John, what's happening?"

"I'm done."

"Done with what?"

"With my job. With this life."

"What does that mean?"

"It means I'm done." And with that, my father started the car and backed out of the driveway.

We didn't see him for four days.

That night, when Key and I were eight, after our father gave us gifts and asked for a drink, the night I wet myself, he left. He wouldn't answer his phone. He made no effort to contact us.

Gone.

My mother, maybe terrified he'd left for good, could only wait. Four days, as far as Key and I could tell, my mother went without sleep, without food.

My father showed up, finally, without warning, at dinner. He came through the front door to the table. He was a mess. His eyes red, his mouth bent, his face unshaven. Wild, dirty, and devastated. He wouldn't sit down. He wouldn't talk.

My mother came alive, alert, exhausted as she was, and frightened. She waited for my father to say something, but Key spoke first.

"Dad?" Key's gentlest voice. "Do you want to eat with us?"

Silence. I could hear my father's teeth grinding.

"John?" My mother.

My father had been leaning on a chair, and he picked it up, smashed it down.

"I'm," he said and stopped.

My mother, Key, and I waited. All of us silent. We couldn't know what would come next.

"I made a terrible mistake," my father said. "And now I don't know what to do."

My father had always claimed he would love my mother beyond the grave. He'd agreed to raise children. Twins! My father, who had been a painter before he turned to law, thought family life would agree with him. He got rid of his art, tossed out his paints and his brushes and whatever else. He wanted nothing more than to live as a husband and father. And he lied to himself about all of it, maybe even about loving my mother.

No, not that.

"I got everything wrong," he whispered. "It's all out of whack."

"Where have you been?" My mother, leaning on the dining-room table, maybe to hold herself up.

"I don't know," my father said. "Doesn't matter."

"Why don't you sit down and eat?" My mother approached and touched my father's shoulder.

He jolted.

"Get away from me. Stay away from me."

I pushed out my chair, stood up, and my father looked at me, then at Key. Then back to me. I was eight.

"Are you ready to fight your father?" His eyes on me, not exactly angry, not safe, though.

"John." My mother again. "Sit down."

She reached for my father, and he tolerated her hand.

"Sit down, okay? No one wants trouble. You're home. Eat."

My father sat. I sat. My mother sat. We ate.

Not a word among us.

Then my father put down his napkin, got up from the table, and came around to me.

"Stand up," he said. "Let's go, Konrad. Stand up."

"John —" What could my mother do? "John, sit down. Or if you can't, then —"

"Then what, Diane? Not another word."

I put down my fork and stared into my plate. I was shaking with rage, with fear. Why didn't I pee myself then?

"Stand up, Rad. Now."

And I stood.

I was eight, and my father was an angry, ruined god. Somehow our house disappeared, and my mother and my brother dissolved. Just the two of us, my dad and me alone, facing each other on some terrible ground, like the ground under our back porch, dirt and rocks and crabgrass, but it stretched in all directions. My father the god, a sudden giant, glowing with a bright black light.

I couldn't look at him, not directly. I might have burst into flames.

My father hugged me. That's how I remember it. He hugged me like a bear, without love. He meant to crush me, to suffocate me against his chest, and I had no choice. I had to fight.

My father and I wrestled twice in my life. This was the first time.

My father and I wrestled. And as we wrestled, I cried. I shouted. I kicked. I broke all my teeth. My bones exploded. My heart died. My tongue fell out. My hair turned white. I cried, and I begged him to let me go. To let us all go. To leave us alone.

We wrestled through the night, hours and hours. And then he carried me, my whole shattered self, somewhere. I couldn't make it out.

And I slept.

■

My father, John Schoe, simply gave up his life. He stopped being a husband and father. He stopped going to work. He stopped talking to Key and me, and he barely said anything at all to our mother, at least in front of my brother and me. He stopped dealing with the house, with repairs. He drove only when he left the house, and he left without telling anyone where he was going.

What can you do with someone like that?

My father took all of our attention. He took up almost all the air in our house for himself. All three of us ended up walking around him as if he were a rotting carcass or a sinkhole or a patch of quicksand. At the same time, we had to take care of him, get him food, persuade him to clean himself up, to stand, to eat.

Key and I never understood what happened in my father. His unhappiness, invisible to the rest of us, must have grown in him like a cancer for years before he turned everything upside down. Maybe he was unhappy all along, his whole life, before Key and I were born, before he gave up painting for the law, before he met our mother. Who knows?

His unhappiness must have gotten deeper even as the rest of us — my mother, Key, and I — thought we were happy, juggling, jumping up and down on the big bed, eating pie, walking a mile backward, on and on. We didn't know anything. Not a thing.

After my father left his job and abandoned his responsibilities, my mother filled the void. She'd always worked, even before my father turned off, saying it was good for her brain and heart to get out of the house, be productive. But she'd had to add a second job, and just before she died, about six months after my father gave up, she started going to school to get her college degree. I don't think my mother could be sure what would happen with my father, whether or not he planned a permanent retirement from the world. She had herself, two children, and an adult — not a husband, not a third child, not a friend or boarder, someone unknowable — to feed and clothe. My mother had to work.

Over seven months, my mother got exhausted, rundown, unhappy. Key and I couldn't know for sure what happened when our parents disappeared into their bedroom at the end of the night. They spoke in whispers. Or my mother whispered, and our father growled.

Our father seemed to save his energy until night, when he could keep our mother awake with his anger at the end of her long days. I imagined his murmured threats of violence if she made moves to get rid of him, divorce or move out, taking us with her. Our mother seemed to respond only with silence. As if she were caught out in the open by a hailstorm and could only hunker down, cover her head. At some point our father would finally leave her alone, finally allow her to sleep.

I would sometimes come out of sleep when I felt the wake behind him, cold and hot at the same time as he passed my room and headed downstairs. He spent the nights doing, far as I knew, nothing at all.

Our mother had had no choice but to become the sole earner to keep us all afloat. She cleaned offices after hours, cleaned houses during the days, and worked part-time at a dollar store. All this while trying to get a degree as quickly as she could in nursing. She couldn't take time from work or studying to hang around with Key and me. When she did stay home, she would make dinner, and she would try hard to laugh with us, to catch up, to listen to our stories, but she would fall asleep early in her clothes, sometimes on the couch, sometimes in bed. Sometimes our father would wake her roughly, poking her shoulder or thigh to get her out of her clothes and into bed. And to talk at her, complain at her, rant at her.

The night Key and I turned nine — I'll never forget it. Her heartbreak and tiredness. And our father was nowhere to be found.

"I miss being a mommy."

"But we have cake," Key said. "And you made it."

She gave us a half-smile. "I'm tired, and I miss you both so much."

What could Key and I say to that?

"We love you," Key said.

"We miss you every day," I said. "We know what you have to do."

"But this isn't what being kids should be about. Looking after yourselves every day. Making dinner out of cans and boxes for you and your dad."

Key and I shrugged. We did look after ourselves. We learned to do our laundry and take care of the garbage, and we cleaned in our way. But we were eight, nine, and we couldn't do enough.

Key said, "We can't make money."

"No," my mother smiled. "But you two, with all those brains. You'll be just fine."

Key and I had sometimes talked about running away, but that meant we would leave our father behind to torture our mother. So we'd talked about how much easier it would be for our mother if we'd never been born, if she could kick out our father and find her own way without us. I was ashamed for being alive. Key, too. Our poor, trapped, exhausted mother.

And on the night of our ninth birthday, with our mother sad and tired, cleaning up our birthday cake, I said, "You must hate us because all the work's for us."

My mother sat stunned for a minute or two, fidgeting with a candle in the shape of a number nine, her eyes darting back and forth between Key and me.

"It's true," Key said. "If you didn't have us, maybe you'd have a new, better husband. And a better life."

My mother pulled us both in. "Life doesn't go like that," she said. "It has its demands. We do what we have to for love. You can't argue with love, and you can't ask it why. It won't answer. Love is the only answer to itself. Do you understand?"

I don't think Key and I understood at all, the idea, I mean, or its depth. But we could sense our mother was saying she would do whatever she could for us, including our father, because she had to, for love.

After a few moments, we nodded, my twin brother and I, in unison.

Four months later, a truck lost a wheel.

FOUR

I'm not the only kid whose grades drop through the floor with trouble at home. I think I peaked in third grade.

I'm not good with school, not since my father gave up and my mother died. I'm not made for structure, rules, authority, or classmates. I've only ever enjoyed learning on my own. I'm really good at teaching myself. I love museums, encyclopedias, Project Gutenberg, and I —

I'll graduate from high school, but I won't show up for graduation. I won't have friends to miss, and you won't find my picture in the yearbook. I'll get my diploma in the mail, maybe, if anyone knows where to reach me.

Eleven months from now, I'm going to enter a monastery. The Lérins Abbey, in France. To live *in* the world but not *of* the world.

Wait. What?

Constant rules, structure, authority, community? With my mind and moods? Totally ridiculous, right? Did I mention the men, the work, and the discipline?

And does Key know about this?

Key, of course, does not know. And this will be the hardest part of the plan, leaving my brother. Key will be somewhere like Princeton or Columbia or Berkeley, or wherever the scholarships let him go. That's the truth of it. Between the two of us, my twin has a chance to light up the world. Key is a good person in almost every way, and I'm not. My light is black.

So, with black light, I will serve God and Christ at a French monastery.

?!

I've never been to church, and I don't know if our parents had us baptized or christened. I don't know anything about God or Christ or Catholicism. I'd have to read up on doctrine. But I have a year.

You might not know where to find the monastery of Lérins.

The monastery is on an island ...

a little island ...

the largest of a tiny archipelago ...

off the coast of the French Riviera ....

What's not to like?

So, Rad, did it occur to you they might not want you, or that you might hate it? Don't you realize you'll commit to a celibate life among men living in relative silence? And how are you going to commit to Christ, someone you know only by name? Doesn't sound like a plan.

Yeah. Not a great plan, maybe not even a good plan. Still, right now, it's a plan. It's a plan to escape, a plan to hide myself from the world.

■

I might not have considered Lérins if not for my co-lossal failure with Jacqui. A failure that began when we began — a long, slow failure that reached its final end this morning.

Maybe. Maybe it's totally dead, maybe it's not.

I should just tell the story. It's a story of ways a person can become an island.

Jacqui Pahk-Morris and I didn't start out friends. We sat near each other in eighth-grade science, and I couldn't keep my eyes off her. I also couldn't find a way to talk to her or be nice or even polite.

Eighth grade was the fifth year of my father's near total absence, though he never actually left. My mother had been dead almost four years. I didn't have much motivation to do anything. I squeaked through all my classes except for math. I intuit math. It comes to me without thinking. Or at least it feels that way. Jacqui couldn't compete with me in math. Don't get me wrong. She was good, really good, but she had to work at it, and I didn't.

Science was different, at least what passed for science in eighth grade. I didn't have the same instincts as with math, and I would have had to work to do well. I didn't work, so I didn't do well. Jacqui had me beat.

This is boring. The history matters, though.

Jacqui and I never spoke to each other, but I looked and looked when I thought she wouldn't notice. And I have to admit, I don't really know why I was looking. At fourteen, she was skinny. Her legs were too long, her face too small for her head, and her hands and feet might have belonged to someone twice as tall and even thinner. She was a collection of parts, not quite put together.

Yeah, maybe, but I had some shadowy idea she was already modeling, which, I have to admit, I couldn't understand. She was awkward. Or I thought she was, but what did I know? Nothing.

What Jacqui had was unbelievable skin. Her skin still is luminous. That's the word, good for a few points on the SAT. Luminous, as if she were lit from the inside by a hundred candles.

And what about Jacqui's eyes? Her eyes weren't quite round or hooded, but not quite not-round or not-hooded, not quite black, not quite brown, not quite, in some light, deep blue.

Now, at seventeen, Jacqui is spectacular in every way. Brains and beauty. She'll go Ivy League like Key, if she really decides to give up the runway. That spectacular. But when she was in eighth grade, she was two inches taller than me, and she wasn't quite —

Her tongue. Her tongue had cracks in it. It wasn't smooth. Weird, right? Like her tongue was the bed of a dried-up river. I never understood that. She can wear anything, cutting-edge fashion with feathers, fur, plastic, leather, silk, wool, yarn, probably bone, the skin of a unicorn, and headdresses you can't even imagine. Or she can go half-naked. Let's face it, though, she'll never be a tongue model.

The first time Jacqui spoke to me, I had just put my hand through the window of the door to our homeroom, which also served for English. Ms. Melonian was my homeroom and English teacher. She wanted to have it entered on my permanent record that I was hostile and volatile, dangerous. She wore red lipstick, red nail polish, red clothes. I called her the Blood Queen.

I showed up late to English, and the Blood Queen confronted me in front of the class. She shouted. I shouted. She shouted some more, maybe even screeched, raised her arm in some kind of incantation, and then I left, but not before punching out a pane of glass in the door. I shouted obscenities in the hallway.

I ended that day with a bandaged hand, detention, and a call to my absentee father, who never answered, but none of this happened before Jacqui Pahk-Morris spoke to me.

Jacqui came out of the girls' bathroom in time to watch me punch an ugly bulletin board hanging in the hallway.

"Ow."

That's the first word Jacqui ever said to me.

I stood in front of her, my fists clenched, oozing blood, snorting like a bull, wondering if I should throw her up in the air on my horns, gore her.

"That must have hurt." She crossed her arms on

her chest, and for a second I stared at her hands, those long, long fingers. They were the fingers of a creature from a parallel world. "Did it hurt?"

— heavy breathing, snorting —

"Konrad?" And that one word, my full name, brought me crashing down from the height of anger.

"What?" My first word to Jacqui. None of this was what anyone would call promising.

"You just punched a bulletin board. Did it hurt?"

"No."

"Your hand is bleeding."

At that point, the Blood Queen came out of the classroom. "Jacqui, come here. Leave him alone."

Jacqui stuck out her tongue, her cracked tongue, to wet her lips a little.

"Go to the nurse," she whispered. "For your hand. And then go to the office. Turn yourself in."

"Jacqui, leave him. Konrad, you have thirty seconds to get yourself to the office."

Jacqui and I looked at each other. I felt my sadness come over me, that heavy blanket.

"First, go sit on the stairs," Jacqui said. "Sit somewhere. Calm down. And then —"

"The office," I said. "I know."

"Jacqui?" The Blood Queen walked a few steps toward us and my anger flared again. I looked at her over Jacqui's shoulder and she stopped.

What chance did the Blood Queen have against an animal like me, spells or not?

"You'll be okay," Jacqui said, and she put her hand on me. That touch was a long drink of warm milk, and all I wanted was to rest. How could I know she wouldn't touch me again, not in any real way, for almost three years? "We'll talk tomorrow."

■

We didn't talk the next day. Or the day after. Or anytime soon.

Jacqui and I fell back into our silence, and I went back to looking at her. Though she started, I think, looking back at me.

Maybe two weeks went by until Jacqui caught up to me after school. She had and has more courage than I will ever possess.

"How's your hand?"

Silence.

"You really, really don't like talking, do you?"

I shrugged.

"I bet I can get you to say more than two words."

"You'd lose."

Pause. You know, to let it sink in.

"Oh," she smiled. "Funny. Is your hand all right?"

I rubbed my hand. "It's fine," I said.

"Rad?"

I waited.

"Rad?"

"Present."

"Wow. Again with the funny."

"Not really."

"Rad?"

"Jacqui?" I had never said her name, and it felt sticky and sweet on my lips, like cotton candy.

"Rad, I've spent some time thinking about this. I think we should be friends."

Silence. I was tasting her name, the taste of blue.

"What do you think? Interested?"

"Why?"

"Why what?"

"Why do you want to be friends with me?"

Jacqui rocked back and forth on her feet. "Don't be stupid," she said.

"That's hard for me," I said.

I walked her home. Jacqui talked, and I listened. Month after month, through the rest of eighth grade, the next summer, and all the way through ninth grade, I walked Jacqui home after school, and then walked the two miles back to my house. And I left my house early every morning to walk the two miles to Jacqui's to walk her to school. I didn't have the money to do anything with her, or nothing more than buy a soda, maybe a slice of pizza, as we walked. I walked her between home and school twice a day, every day, and we talked. We laughed. It all went great. Beautiful. We were friends.

We were friends.

Nothing ever happened. I'm not entirely sure why.

We loved each other, but somehow we couldn't ever touch each other. We didn't hug. We didn't hold hands. We had this unspoken understanding that we wouldn't try. As if there was some kind of barrier, a force field, an invisible fence, something that would repel our hands, give us a painful shock if we attempted it.

Honestly, I think we wanted each other so much we couldn't imagine what would happen to us if we tried to make it real. I think we both thought we would die. Like a mortal taking in a god — *theophany* — which almost never goes well for the mortal.

We laughed. We talked. We didn't touch each other.

We were best friends.

Until we weren't.

■

The summer between ninth and tenth grade, Jacqui went to, of all things, a sleep-away debate camp. Seriously. She researched and argued every day, morning, noon, and night for an entire month of summer. Does that even make sense? We sent each other letters — for some reason, campers weren't allowed to use e-mail — and we talked on the phone ten, fifteen times over the first week.

Then, silence.

The letters from Jacqui stopped. The phone calls stopped. Nothing.

Emptiness.

The silence drove me wild with worry, anger, desire. I went into some kind of chemical withdrawal, and I could barely stand up for all the pain in my body. Maybe you know what I mean. Fullness, then emptiness, then sickness.

For nine days I was nothing but a vicious storm at home. Key couldn't speak to me, look at me. He was more like the National Guard than my brother, the militia protecting the citizenry and their property from my weather, trying to work against the wind and rain and flooding.

But the storm was indoors and out, and there was nowhere for Key to hide.

And then Jacqui called. Jacqui called, and for a moment all the weather lifted.

Jacqui called, and with that call everything ended. My weather and my heart. Ended for real.

An island in the making.

"So, Rad," Jacqui said. "There's this guy."

That's all she needed to say. But I was her best friend, so I clenched my fists and my teeth, fought the desire to throw up, or hang myself, or reach through the phone, and I said, "Does this guy have a name?"

"It doesn't matter."

This landed between us, and I knew the whole story. That one sentence, "It doesn't matter," sat there between us, like a severed head in a sack. Know what I mean? A murder had occurred, a crime, something ugly and terrible, and there wasn't anything we could do about it. No going back. I mean, we had this head between us, and someone had to pick it up.

"Why?"

"Why what, Rad?"

"Why doesn't it matter?"

This time Jacqui didn't have the words.

Silence. Then I erupted.

"Why didn't you call me, Jacqui? I'm your best friend. Why didn't you call me? I would have talked you out of it. I would have talked you out of him, out of doing what you did, out of everything. I would've stopped you. I could've stopped you."

"That's why I didn't call."

Jacqui had hit me with a hammer. My best friend. A hammer. I shook my head to come to my senses.

"What do you mean?" I think I growled it, sneered it.

"I didn't want you to talk me out of anything."

"I can't believe this. How could you have done this to yourself? How could you have done this to me? Didn't you miss me at all? How could sleeping with whatever-his-name-is have ever seemed like the right thing? You're fifteen. *We're* fifteen. And we —"

I couldn't say it.

"We what, Rad?"

"Nothing. Nothing, nothing, nothing."

She heard me punch the chest of drawers in my room.

"Rad? What did you hit?"

I punched the furniture again.

"Rad, stop."

Again, again. Punching.

I hung up.

I hung up, and I thought, *I'm done.*

The wildness, that wildness was different from all the other wildness because love was attached to it. A girl was attached to it. Rejection, jealousy, confusion, helplessness, envy, anger, and sadness.

I was drunk. I wanted to die. So I went to the kitchen.

I wanted a knife. I wanted to stab myself a hundred times, be done with it, with everything. I went to the kitchen. Nine-thirty at night. I wanted the biggest knife I could find, but what I found in the kitchen was —

My father, standing over the kitchen sink. His shoulders hunched. He was alone, staring into the sink. Who knows why?

My father stood between me and the block of old knives barely sharp enough to break the skin. They would work, though. They were still knives. My father stood between me and death, a death I wanted more than anything else.

"Move," I said, and I shoved him.

My father hadn't really been my father for years. He had given up, and then his wife died, and he did nothing but wait for all his money to run out — his own money, his family's — and then he watched his sons work when he didn't. But he was still my father, and he had seen me storm before, though nothing like this. I was a cyclone. I brought high winds and heavy rain and destruction. He hadn't ever seen me with such deep hate for myself.

I shoved him and lunged for the knives. I nearly got my hand on one.

"Rad?" My father put out his arm and stopped me cold. "What's up?"

I fought. I tried pushing against him.

"Give me the knife," I said.

"That's not a good idea." He brushed the block of

knives away with one hand and held me off with the other.

"Dad." Frantic. "Give me the knife."

By now, my father actually needed both arms. He didn't want to hurt me. He tried to hold me, but I was putting everything I had against him. It wasn't a fight, though, not really. My father was impossible to conquer. Even though I was fifteen and almost as tall as him, my father kept me off just as he had done when I was eight-almost-nine and wrestled him at the dinner table. All my weather, and he was like one of those massive statues on Easter Island. Immovable and upright after a thousand years of sun and rain and wind.

"Please," I begged him. "Please, let me have a knife."

"I can't do that, Rad."

"Please," I said, and then everything drained out of me, and I slumped to the floor. "Please let me die."

My father settled down next to me on the floor. He held his knees in his arms. He might have been breathing heavy, at least a little.

He waited.

Then, for the first time since my mother died, since before my mother died, my father held me.

■

My father kept me from what might have ended with my death. Instead, I woke up in my bed, and I had the embarrassing sense that my father must have carried me, at fifteen, to my room.

Jacqui.

I didn't leave my room for hours. I hoped my father had left the house or gone back into his own head, and I didn't want to see Key.

Jacqui.

"Rad?"

My ghost mother sat at the end of my bed, her hand on my feet. This wasn't the first time she'd sat with me, talked with me.

"What?"

"It's time to stand up."

"Is it?"

"Yes. You can't lie here until you die."

"Maybe I'll just give up. Like Dad."

My mother rubbed my foot. "You know something's happening in your dad. Whatever it is, it's different from what you're feeling. About Jacqui, I mean."

Jacqui.

My mother disappeared.

"All right," I said.

I had to leave my room to get out of my own stink. I went to the kitchen, and there was my father, standing over the sink as if he had never left but to get me to bed. Maybe he hadn't.

"Key's out shopping. For groceries." He poured me a glass of milk and handed it to me. "How're you feeling?"

Jacqui.

"Hungover." I drank the milk. My father poured more. "Don't tell Key," I said. "Please."

"Tell Key what?" he said.

Maybe he was protecting me. I had no idea. Who knows if he remembered anything at all of my fight for the knives.

■

Lérins, an island monastery. A tiny community that dates to the fifth century. Filled with monks.

An island of islands.

At times like these I talk to my dead mother, who thinks I could go straight to work writing code, programming, except, as I mentioned, I hate technology. Maybe I hate it because I eat code for breakfast, lunch and dinner. I'm sick of code. I think I'll choke on SQL, even if I try to wash it down with Java.

Two years ago I started to develop my own code, a new code, aRKay, for the letters *R* and *K*, Rad and Key, but I — I got bored. I stopped developing it. Plain old quit.

That's the funny and worst thing about having a talent or vocation as natural to you as breathing. Who gets paid to breathe? We breathe to live, but who lives to breathe?

I breathe. I program. Who cares?

"How lucky you are," my ghost mother says, "to know what you're good at. To have so much talent. To have so much brain."

"How lucky," I say. "I'm designed to sit in front of a machine and type. Wahoo."

"You could be a millionaire by nineteen. You might have been one by now if you wanted."

"Kind of makes me sick to think about it."

"Sick? I died on my way to work, Konrad, cleaning offices and homes. I got hit by a tire. If I'd had your brain. Or Key's."

"You do. Did."

"No, I didn't. I'm old enough to know. But you? Time spent with a computer — you could change the world. Who are you to say, Nah, it's boring? That's selfish."

"I think I'll enlist."

"Oh, because the US Army doesn't have computers? Do you have the discipline for that, the emotional stability? Can you be shouted at all day without coming apart? Do you want to shoot someone or get shot? For what?"

"Defending our nation against the forces of evil?"

"Not funny."

"How about the Navy?"

My mother shakes her head in disbelief.

"Coast Guard?"

"Honestly, Rad, are you that dense? Computers live everywhere. No matter where you go, you will meet a computer."

"I can hide."

"No, Rad, you can't. You're not a coward."

My dead mother waits, her eyes fixed on my eyes until I look away.

"Unless, of course, you are."

∎

"Coward." That's what Jacqui called me just this morning, sometime before Key went to my father on the platform, before my father died.

"Seriously, Rad. You're afraid of everything."

"Am I?"

"Yes." She pulled her bag over her shoulder. "You're afraid of me, at least, afraid of anything that has to do with love."

I remembered our first kiss, last year. I owed it to Key.

My brother, as he told me months later, was at Jacqui's house visiting Harrison, Jacqui's older brother. Honestly, Key spent more time there than I ever did, since I pretty much said hello and goodbye at the door, back when I walked Jacqui to and from school.

"I know how you can get Rad to give in," Key said to Jacqui.

"Give in?"

"Surrender. Give up. To you."

"Oh? How's that?"

"You don't believe me?"

"I don't know," Jacqui said. "You're his twin, so if anyone knows his secret, you do. But I think he's haunted, Key, and he doesn't want to hurt me."

"He is haunted, and he's brilliant, and he's seriously twisted up. But he loves you."

"I know. I have almost three years of curiosity burning my brain. Your brother. There's no figuring him out."

"Islands," Key said.

"I know all about the islands."

"But it's more than that, Jacqui. Islands make sense to him."

"Talking about Rad?" Harrison had come in and kissed my brother. "He's something else."

"Watch it," Key said. "He's my brother."

"What? I like the kid, always have. I mean, I'd trust him with my sister's life."

"Okay," Jacqui said. "We all love Rad, but how do I get him to kiss me? Or even walk with me again?"

Harrison laughed. "Can you make any sense of this? A girl like Jacqui can't get to your brother? He's made of iron. Seriously. Or maybe he's the one who's fluid."

"No," Key said, kissing Harrison's cheek. "That's definitely me."

"Hello?" Jacqui said. "You were saying something, Key. Islands?"

Key turned back to Jacqui. "Just tell him a kiss is the bridge between islands."

Jacqui shook her head. "That's it?"

"Tell him you're both islands in a common sea, something like that, and that he's closer to you than he thinks. Then tell him again. A kiss is the bridge."

"You and your brother are romantics," Harrison said. "Twin souls."

"That's us, sweetheart," Key said, putting his hand on Harrison's chest.

Harrison left for college a few months later, and Key, who had put what he had into Jacqui's brother, would end up abandoned, adrift.

A couple of days later, Jacqui found me at school.

"Walk me home," she said.

"It's been a long time."

"And I've missed you. So walk me home."

We walked without speaking. I didn't know what to say, so I waited.

Finally, on a quiet block, Jacqui said, "I know you think about islands, memorize them, and when you're upset, you visit them in your head."

"You've been talking to Key."

"I have, but it doesn't matter. You and I, Rad, we're islands. Your mom died. Your father isn't a father. Your brain works how it works, and your heart. So you're really alone." Jacqui stopped walking. "I'm alone, too. My life, right? Modeling, debate, science. But we've been floating so close to each other for years, right next to each other."

Silence.

"I think it's time to find the bridge between us, Konrad."

"What's going on?" I said. "What do you mean?"

"I think we have to go under the water to find the bridge that connects us."

Jacqui was talking to my lips, and finally I woke up. Somewhere inside of me, a spark landed in dry tinder.

"I loved you, and you didn't wait for me," I said. "You were the one who didn't think much of us."

Jacqui sighed. "You're talking about debate camp? Forever ago?"

"A year and a half, not forever. And yes, it still hurts. All I wanted was you."

"You never told me that."

"I didn't think I had to. I walked with you every day. Two miles to pick you up, two miles after I dropped you off. Why did I have to say anything?"

Jacqui lowered her eyes. "When will you forgive me?"

"For being blind and hurting me?"

"Yes, for that."

"I don't know." I kicked at a pebble. "You let someone else build a bridge to you."

She nodded. "I know, but that's just it, that bridge was man-made."

"Wow, Jac. Don't remind me."

"No. I mean it was artificial, weak from the beginning, and it fell down."

"But you wanted that bridge."

Jacqui shook her head. "You're really going to make me work for this."

"What does that mean?" I felt myself clenching my teeth. My heart caught fire. "I just don't understand. You chose someone else before me."

"Okay. I'm sorry." Jacqui took a deep breath. "Everybody thinks they want the easy bridge, the bridge that lasts just long enough and then falls. But, Rad — the bridge between us is a land bridge. It's under the water and not too deep. You can almost see it through the waves. We've always had it. We're already bridged."

Jacqui leaned into me.

We kissed.

We kissed, and for a moment I felt like I was becoming an island, a high island, a true island made of lava. An undersea volcano gave me up to the ocean and waves, and I broke through to the air. I was hotter than I'd ever been, and cool. Steam and rock. Molten and solid.

We kissed, and I was Atlantis, the island city lost to water, submerged, and then raised up from the bottom of the ocean to the surface by some Titan.

Jacqui and I, kissing, became an island in the street, and the people had to pass around us, break for us, like waves.

The tides fell away. Or we were raised up high enough to see the land that connected us. We were joined, and we went back and forth to each other.

I was more an island than ever before — and less.

■

But it couldn't last. The ocean rose, and our bridge drowned.

I'm talking about the ocean in me. The ocean of fear and sadness and daydreams and whatever else.

The dark ocean I had known since before my mother died.

I had no idea what to do with Jacqui.

"You have no idea what to do with me," Jacqui said this morning.

"That's not exactly true," I said. "I like looking at you."

"I know you do."

"I like touching you, too." Jacqui still had her luminous skin, but —

Imagine touching something you're not entirely sure you *are* touching. I mean, you can feel something solid under your hand, but you can't detect anything on the surface to prove you're not only stroking air. I think some fur is like this. Chinchilla, maybe. When I touch Jacqui — touched, past tense — I sometimes felt I wasn't touching a person, touching skin, touching anything at all. Except Jacqui *is* a real, human girl. Strange, really, to love a girl who's almost an illusion of a girl.

"Touching you might sometimes be better than looking at you," I said.

"Not exactly grounds for a relationship," Jacqui said.

"I'm better at talking now than I ever was," I said. "Remember when I could barely talk at all?"

"Yes, but —"

"You're not happy. I hate that you're not happy."

"Who's happy, Rad? Really, who's ever happy?"

"Shouldn't you be happy? You have everything."

"Do I? I'll go to college, and I have plenty of money, but modeling's finally gotten too stupid and unbelievably stressful. You really have no idea. You never have. Except that you wonder if I'll come home from wherever I have to go. You wonder who I'm with, what I'm doing, and it eats you up. I love you, and you have no way of holding on to that. You can barely talk to me, since you can't sort through your feelings and ideas long enough to make sense of what you want. You'll escape high school, and then what? You won't code or surrender to what you can do, so? And I can't complain about anything without you getting all nuts on me. I just want you to listen, but you can't stand it when I'm — I don't know."

"Unhappy. My mother was unhappy."

But Jacqui had stopped listening.

"My brother, Harrison, dropped off the face of the earth, sort of. He never calls, texts, nothing, and he never comes home. He abandoned me, my parents, not just Key. Key can't look me in the eye. He can't talk to me. The two of you. And —"

"Tolstoy."

Jacqui stared at me. Her bluebrownblack eyes wild. "Tolstoy?"

"Forget it."

"Coward."

That word.

"Just like your father. He gave up his wife and kids but couldn't find anything else to do. Your mother died, and —"

Why did she have to mention my mother? The fire in my heart.

"I'm not a coward." How could I tell Jacqui the only thing that made sense was to be by myself or spend the rest of my life with her, trying to make her happy? I wanted to give myself to an island far away from everyone and everything, or live on the island Jacqui and I would make for ourselves. "I'm seventeen, and I don't know what to do with everything inside me."

"Coward. Seriously, Rad, you're afraid of everything."

That's when I burst into flames.

"Am I?" I snarled.

"Yes." Jacqui pulled her bag up onto her shoulder. She couldn't look in my face. I would have burnt her eyes. I was fire. "You're afraid of me, at least, afraid of anything that has to do with love."

"I'm afraid of truck tires coming loose," I growled. "I'm afraid my father will take a swan dive off that platform he built."

"Quite an image. But I'm not talking about truck tires or your father. I'm talking about you and love. We love each other, and you won't let it happen. You won't let it grow. You're worried all the time, every second."

I wish my dead mother could have shown up this morning to talk me down, to talk to Jacqui. I wish she could have told my girlfriend to walk with me and let me find my balance. I wish —

"Look at me," I said. My heart crackling, burning black. "You have the courage to call me names, to talk about my dead mother and tell me what I'm afraid of, then you have the courage to look at me. We're done, Jacqui. We're islands on opposite sides of the world."

■

The irony of being extremely emotional — angry, if that's what you want to call it, since anger always speaks the loudest — is that my emotions —

Put it this way. I feel and don't feel at the same time.

No. That's not true.

I feel sad, always sad, even when I'm angry. I'm sure it's not really me who's spinning away out of control. I mean, it's me, Konrad Schoe, but it's not me. There's a difference between what my soul experiences and what my mind experiences. I feel as if I have to watch a second me feeling and doing all the wrong things. I watch myself out of control. I watch myself punching walls, laughing like a maniac, throwing glass pitchers full of water, threatening the one person I want to love, drunk with emotion. I say to myself, No, don't. I say, Come back from the edge. I say, Stop.

Stop, Rad. Stop, stop, stop.

No.

Please?

No.

I keep going and going until I'm drained, until I'm sober and straight. I have to watch myself helpless with my emotions. I have to feel ashamed. And sad.

I don't know if you can understand what this experience does to a person over time, especially if you're not the kind of person who loses your self-control. Try to imagine or remember a time when you watched your life pass by, when you didn't feel in control of your own experience, when maybe someone else made all the decisions. Did you ever have anyone take control of your life, even for a little while? Have you ever felt helpless to stop a car when you wanted it stopped? Have you ever been tickled or held hostage? Felt tormented by something you couldn't figure out?

The difference is that I have to take responsibility for everything I say and do, even when I have no control over myself. I always have to take responsibility for how I hurt or upset or anger other people, or for how I embarrass myself in public and private. I always have to answer for something.

People who have rough minds actually feel more responsibility for what they are — and aren't — than people who don't have rough minds.

Seriously. Who's more responsible and less responsible at the same time than a total lunatic?

It's tiring. I'm seventeen, and for most of my life I've been praying to a god I don't understand or know, a stranger god, to let me get some control over my heart and mind. That god never listens, never helps. I have asked that god to kill me, to let me die, and that god won't let me get out of the world.

So does this mean I ever get to be a coward? Do I get to make excuses or run from what I am and what I say? Can I blame someone else? My father? Key? Jacqui? This person or that person? Gods or devils?

No. I feel what I feel, do what I do, say what I say. There's just me. Even if it isn't me.

In my soul I'm not angry. In my soul I'm not out of control. In my soul I want peace.

But everyone will tell you I'm angry, I'm uncontrollable, I'm unsafe.

I think about going to that monastery to get some peace. Maybe the god I need for help lives on an island off the coast of France. Maybe it'll be the monks who save me. Or the lonesomeness.

I want to go to let other people off the hook. They won't have to walk on eggshells. They won't have to worry.

That's it, too, right? The worry the people who might love me or like me could feel. The fear. When will I get angry at a person who will kick the crap out of me? When will I throw myself in front of a bus or —

Lose my mind for good?

Or, as Key said, when will I die from fighting with my own emotions, my own mind and heart?

Get hold of yourself, Rad. Get hold of yourself.

A monastery would be like quarantine. It would be a place to go that would keep me and everyone else out of harm's way. Maybe.

I could be quiet there.

And it's on an island.

FIVE

Imagine a person struck with a deadly sickness, an awful cancer. And, then, to everyone's surprise: remission. Happiness. The sick one wakes up full of life, better than ever, and they act as if they haven't just been suffering — or that you weren't suffering with their suffering. They get up, walk, eat, go to work, see a movie. They don't want to talk about what they missed. They don't want to talk about the pain. They don't want to talk about what will happen if they get worse again. They want to live.

My father didn't have cancer. He wasn't terminally ill. He had made a choice.

He decided to give up on life before my mother died. After my mother died, he didn't change his mind. He didn't say to himself, "My wife is gone. My children need me. My house needs attention. I'm up for it."

Nope.

The house fell into disrepair. Little things at first — dripping faucets and loose doors and scummy walls, a blackgreen bathroom, the annoyances and blemishes and dirt and grime people put up with without much complaining, aware that it all should be better, but with no real motivation to keep up, especially when at the center of the home there's a sense of hopelessness.

Our house, now a dangerous eyesore, an embarrassment among the five other houses on our neat dead end, wasn't always that way.

Neglected. On and on, slow decay.

When the roof started to go, three years after my mother died, when Key and I were twelve, when the weather came in, dripping and streaming down through rotten shingles, overhead lights, and seams in the ceilings, and when my brother and I lost our limited ability to keep up with cleaning — Key and I only did the laundry and cooking without knowing what more we should or could do — we confronted my father. It took all our courage, but he surprised us.

Our father seemed to want to live again.

You wouldn't call our father a handy man, but he was no fool. Over three or four days, he read from a book on home repair. He stripped and patched and retiled the roof. And this somehow returned him to us for a spell. He moved around the house from this repair to that, cleaning, tightening, scraping, scrubbing, hammering. Doing. He made dinner once. A couple of times he drove Key and me to school or work, on errands here and there.

Key went to my father like a kitten to a bowl of milk. But I held out.

Once, as if he knew he had Key in his hand, my father put his hand on his shoulder, a gesture that passed for affection, and said, "Key." Almost like he might have said, "I love you."

"Where you going now?" Key asked him.

"Rehang the basement door."

That door hadn't swung right since the house had begun to collapse and the foundation give way.

"Does it make any sense?" I asked my brother when we were alone.

"What? Dad?"

"He just shows up because we asked him to? He's a dad all of a sudden, able to do everything we need?"

"Just like when we were little."

"That's what I'm saying, Key. He's been gone a long time. Mom's been gone a long time. And now look."

"It's been days," Key said. "He's happy, so I'm happy."

"I just don't understand. There's a lot I don't get."

"Like what?"

"We don't know what he's really thinking, or if he's really back. He hasn't even mentioned Mom. He hasn't talked about anything in years."

"But he's here, and he seems like Dad."

"Seems."

"Okay. He *is* Dad."

"I don't like it," I said. "He sounds like Dad. He looks like Dad. But who is he?"

"Dad," Key said.

"I know it won't last. But it's good to pretend he's here now. Dad being Dad."

Those eleven days, when our father fixed the roof and worked around the house, when he seemed to come alive, I resisted him —

It took me a little while, but my father finally lured me, too. And he lured me with a globe.

■

One of the reasons I had loved my father so much, until everything fell apart, until he abdicated, until my mother died —

He had a way with me, a way of calming me down. He was a Rad whisperer. I don't know how he did it. He was a quiet guy, not really one for talking much. He didn't laugh a lot. He didn't really like to be hugged or touched, at least not by Key and me. Only our mother could touch him whenever she wanted. He tolerated Key's and my hugs, but I never thought he actually enjoyed them. He almost never touched us, instead waiting for us to go to him. Maybe he worried he would be too rough. He was a big man, but not enormous. He acted, though, as if his hands were made of concrete, as if he would hurt us even when he tried to be gentle.

My father's number-one quality before everything went sideways? He loved our mother. He loved her with everything inside of him. You could see it in his eyes, and you could see it in how he carried himself around her, as if he didn't want his size or bulk to take any of the air that belonged to her. He loved her every second of every day, and we knew he would die for her. Key and I knew he would die for us, too. We trusted him. We trusted him right up until the time when we couldn't.

I trusted him. He made sure my brother and I were safe and comfortable in little and big ways, like fixing us tea — all of this way before Mom died — or bringing us glasses of water or mixing up oatmeal. He vacuumed our rooms and washed our clothes. He took us to the doctor. He cared for us. He never let up. He cared all the time. From the moment he woke up to the moment he went to sleep. I think he thought about us even in his sleep, in his dreams. His love for us seemed infinite.

When I was nine, the year Mom died, I fell in love with magic. Once, on one of the rare days when my mother had the energy to take us out, Key and me, we stopped in a coffee shop for a few minutes to use the bathroom. While I waited, I found an audience in an old man who was just minding his own business. I must have shown him four or five simple little tricks, my whole repertoire, and then my mother came with Key.

"Oh, gosh," my mother said. "Has my son been bothering you?"

"No, no," the man said. "Not at all. He's a very charming boy, and he's been showing me his magic."

"Has he?" My mother smiled down at me. "Well,

we'll take the show on the road."

"One moment," said the man. He fished a handkerchief from his pocket. "Hold out your hand, son."

I held out my hand.

"You'll agree this is a plain blue handkerchief?" The man showed me both sides of the handkerchief.

I nodded.

"I'm going to fold this handkerchief into the palm of your hand." The man did as he said, folding the handkerchief eight times into a little square. He held it in place with the tip of his finger. "Close up your hand," he said. "A tight fist."

The man waved his hand over my fist, under my fist, and he mumbled a little something, something I couldn't quite hear, but I knew they were powerful and dark words.

"Now," he said, "open up your hand."

When I opened my hand, there was a square of something, but not the handkerchief.

Paper —

"Go ahead," the man said. "Open it up."

I was caught somewhere between happy and frightened, but I opened up the square.

A fifty-dollar bill, one crisp Ulysses Grant. A fortune.

"Mom," I said. "Look."

"That's pretty amazing," my mother said. She wouldn't take the bill. "Now give the money back to the man."

"No," the man said. "It's not mine to take. It belongs to your son. Or to you."

"No, sir, we can't," my mother said. "Please give it back, Rad."

"Madam," said the man. "It's magic. Nothing else."

Could the old man see the three of us were poor and falling apart? Did he see my mother's exhaustion? And how did he turn the handkerchief into money?

"We can't," said my mother, and she seemed now close to tears. Just one more humiliation. Or was it the man's generosity? Or both?

"Yes, you can." The man smiled. "Have a good rest of the day."

I wish the man had vanished in smoke with a snap of his fingers. Instead, he went back to his newspaper, a newspaper I hadn't noticed and couldn't be sure he'd been holding a few minutes earlier.

My mother didn't move for a few seconds. We stood there. The man, though, acted as if we had left, never even existed. Show over.

On our way out, I handed my mother the bill. She slid it into her pocket without a word. Maybe it was there when she died a few weeks later.

All this talk about magic is really about something else. Until I was eight, my father had always left me with the feeling that he'd given me a fortune, left it in the palm of my hand without my noticing. I would clench my fists in anger, upset and wild, and he would pass his hand around me, mumbling something I couldn't make out, and when I opened my fists, I had a fortune. I had a treasure of peace.

But this, like everything else, stopped.

■

My father knew I loved geography and maps and islands. He also knew, maybe felt, I held back from running to him when he suddenly returned to Key and me for those days when he decided to fix up the house and play dad. He'd never been gone, not physically. He'd watched us get run down and stood by as the house fell apart. He would give us a weekly allowance of money out of some last dwindling account for food, enough to eat out of cans. Sardines, salmon, tuna, ham. A loaf of bread. Bananas.

But to lure me back, my father gave me my own globe. He bought me with a model of the world.

It wasn't fancy. Plastic with a cheap metal base, ten inches in diameter and not very detailed, out of date. But I could see the Seychelles and the Canary Islands. I could make out the Faroes.

"Thank you," I said. I couldn't even look at him.

New Guinea, Baffin, Taiwan, the Falklands.

"You're welcome," he said.

The Channel Islands. Cape Breton. And Easter.

"I know you love the world, Rad. And I have a surprise for you."

"What?" The Lesser Antilles and Bermuda. "Another surprise?"

"It's actually a surprise for the three of us, little man. But that globe will mean a great deal more very soon."

Ireland. The Isle of Man. Borneo.

And I loved my father.

I loved him for three days.

■

Two nights after my father gave me the globe, he made us dinner — hot dogs and baked beans — and we ate outside on the long front grass. We didn't sit on our back porch, since my father had been using it and the garage as staging areas for his repairs. Key and my father and I sat on the grass, and we couldn't help but look at our neighbors in the cul-de-sac. The Jayneses, two doors down, had a lush garden, a neat house, and they must have been horrified at what had become of our house in the three years since my mother died, and horrified with the state of our family.

All my life, a stone that reminded me of a slouching giant sat in the front yard of their house. That stone had always frightened me. It could have resembled a gardener stooping in the garden, pulling weeds, watching a worm, stroking a flower. Who knows what? But I saw a troll sharpening an axe or strangling a rabbit, doing something terrible, whatever it was hidden by his broad back. I'd imagine that stone standing to its full height, maybe eight or nine feet, and turning toward me. I couldn't quite make out a face, but it grimaced, that stone, that giant, with all its cruel ugliness.

It had the expression of someone who enjoyed killing, who enjoyed watching an animal or a person suffer.

I scare myself even now.

It was my father who tamed that stone for me.

My father, Key, and I were sitting in the grass, eating dinner together, when my father said, "So, what frightens you most?"

Key and I looked at each other.

"Key?"

My dead mother was sitting with us, holding a hot dog with ketchup and relish and onions. My father had his hand on her knee, and he said, "Tell us, Diane. What are you most afraid of?"

"I don't know," my mother said. "I shouldn't. Saying it is as good as making it come true."

My father smiled. "Nothing will happen by saying it, I promise."

"I sometimes dream Key and Rad will die in front of me. Sometimes they're bleeding, sometimes burning, sometimes going under waves, drowning."

"They're just dreams, honey." My father, in his soothing voice. "Just dreams."

"I know. Here they are, safe and sound. But I'm most afraid of losing my boys while I sit by, helpless."

My father put his rough hand on my dead mother's smooth cheek and said something I couldn't make out. His murmuring was deep and indecipherable. My mother nodded and kissed the palm of his hand.

"It's crazy," she said. "But that's what it means to be frightened. We let our imaginations run wild or —"

Wet ourselves, I guess. My mother never finished the sentence.

"You weren't most afraid of dying and leaving us all alone?" I said this out loud.

My father and brother looked over at me.

"What was that, Rad?" My father.

"Nothing," I said.

My father stared at me a moment, then went back to my brother. "Still thinking, Key? Can't be that hard."

"It's a hard question," Key started. "I'm afraid of things that would happen to Rad — and you. And I'm afraid of what might happen to people I know and don't know. War, bombings, stabbings, shootings, whatever."

My father nodded. "Okay, but what do you never want to face alone, Key?"

My brother closed his eyes and took a deep breath. "God. I don't ever want to face God."

"You're most afraid of God?"

"God or *a* god. What's scarier than a god? I've read myths in school. Greek, Norse. I've even read a little in the Bible. And some Hindu stuff. What about a being that can change you into a dog or a mouse or a flower, anything they want? What's worse than something that can kill you or hurt you just by thinking it? And what does a god even look like? They're too bright for us. We would go blind. Maybe our minds would light on fire, or our hearts. Maybe we would die happier than we can imagine, just by seeing them for a moment, but we would still die. I'm scared of gods."

"What about demons?" my father said. "Which is worse, gods or demons?"

"Gods," Key said without hesitation. "Demons are always bad. So what? But a god *might* make us suffer. Demons don't punish us. The gods punish us. We can never be sure what the gods will do to us."

"God isn't merciful?" my father said. "God isn't love?"

Key closed his eyes, concentrating. He shrugged. "Only a person can be love," he said.

We sat for a little while in silence. I was wondering if a god really was more frightening than a demon, when my brother finally said, "What about you, Dad?"

"I'm most afraid of losing my mind. I'm most afraid of being unable to talk or walk because my mind will stop or dry up or die in a civil war waged inside me."

My brother and I stared at him.

"That's why," our father said. "That's why all of this. That's why I quit."

Key and I waited for more.

"That day when I got into a fight, when I came home. You remember. I had lost control. I had lost control, and I had grown up in a family known for losing its control." My father looked at me, and he looked heartbroken.

Heartbreak. A word much too simple for the SAT, and much deeper than almost any word you can think of, other than, maybe, *love*, which you need to have to feel heartbroken.

My father looked at me as if he saw something in me he wished he didn't see. "I'm from a family that's had its share of madness."

Madness? This was news, and I —

"Do you think you're going crazy?" My brother said it quietly, but he kept his eyes on our father.

"I'm moody," my father said. "I know it."

Moody? Moody means someone who runs hot and cold, or sometimes on and sometimes off. Moodiness didn't explain anything my father had done.

"I gave up the world to control my mind," my father continued. "And after Mom died, that got harder. It took all my attention." My father was upset, and then he changed direction. "My parents died young, both from cancer, and I have an uncle who was institutionalized. If I'm lucky, I'll get to spend a long time with you, the two of you sitting right here."

"Why now?" I blurted it out. "Why are you coming back now?"

My father stared into his hot dog, looking for inspiration, maybe, or for an honest answer. I didn't know if I could trust whatever he said.

"The rain coming through the ceiling," he said. "A leaky ceiling is a metaphor for a mind, and —"

"Dad," Key said, "I think when you asked us what we're scared of, you thought we were going to say ouija boards or killer clowns or cemeteries. Maybe fire, maybe vampires. Maybe witches or rollercoasters."

"I guess so," my father said.

"We're talking about what we're really frightened of."

My father turned to me. "What about you, Rad?"

"I don't know."

"You don't have to go," Key said.

"Yes, he does." My father cleared his throat, a sign of impatience. "Rad?"

My father might lose his mind, if he hadn't lost it more or less already, and my brother might meet a vengeful, capricious god —

"I'm scared of a rock."

Silence.

"A rock?" my father said, and I nodded.

"What rock?" Key said.

"That rock in the Jayneses front yard."

"That?" Key said, pointing down the block.

They both looked.

"I get it," my father said. "It looks like a man, some kind of giant."

"Are you two for real?"

"Have you *looked* at that rock, Key?" My father, defending me. "Come here and take a gander." He stood up and got my brother and me over to our driveway. "From this angle, that thing could be doing anything, and probably something terrible."

"I know," I said. "He could be eating a baby right now."

"Oh, Rad." My mother reappeared. "A baby?"

"And what if he stood up and came this way?"
My father, his hands on his hips, still taller than my
brother and me by a head, and strong. "What could
we do against an enormous man of stone?"

"Nothing," I whispered.

"I've never thought about that rock," Key said.
"But I see what you mean. And I wish I didn't."

"It's really scary," my mother agreed.

"But look a little closer," my father said. "I don't
think we're seeing it right."

I strained to see the stone in some new way, but
I couldn't. It seemed only evil, and I wanted to go
inside and finish my dinner in safety.

"Rad," my father said, "that stone man is injured.
The way the light falls on his shoulder, right now, in
the evening, we can see it. Some kind of deep gash in
his back, under his shoulder blade. That man's bleeding. Maybe stabbed down into his ribs. When I look
at that rock, I see a man who needs to sleep where
he's sitting, to recover from something awful. He's in
pain. He needs to sleep or die."

I had to think about this. My father wasn't stupid. He was talking to a twelve-year-old boy, almost
thirteen, not a little kid. He was appealing to my
compassion, my imagination. And he was talking to
all of us. To my mother, too.

My father made that stone into something we could all think over. He made it into whatever frightened each of us.

Couldn't that stone have an untreatable wound, a mortal wound, making my mother feel helpless? Couldn't that stone be the image of a god, or a man injured by a god, which spooks Key? Couldn't that stone be going crazy with pain, making my father wonder over his own mind? Couldn't that enraged stone still rise up, lash out?

I never looked at that stone the same way again after that. I could only see it as an injured giant, a giant that could fall, but, being a stone, would never fall. And maybe all he could do, that giant, is stare down at the ground in front of him, wanting forever just to lie down.

But today, my father died. And after Key and I figure what to do about that, I'll walk over to look at the stone in the Jayneses yard. I'll see it in a new way. That stone will look nothing at all like a man or a giant. Not anymore. It will look like a simple stone, rough and hard, without the ability to speak or feel or move or break or suffer.

■

My father and his surprises.

The day after our hot-dog dinner in the grass,

exactly three days after he gave me the globe and eight days after his miraculous recovery, he took Key and me aside.

"I've got something cooking. Something big."

"A stunt?" Key said. "Like when we were little?"

"Something like that. Have you been studying your globe, Rad? Do you ever think about the best way to get around the world?"

I didn't know what to say, so I said nothing.

"Well," my father said, bumping my chin with his fist, "I don't know what your problem is, but I'm telling you I've got a very, very long trip planned out."

"A record-setting trip?" Key said.

"I don't know." My father turned to Key. Something in his eyes. My mother? A memory? "It's not a trip for world records, though we could make it one."

This marked a betrayal.

Before my mother died, my parents had always planned together, made things happen together. Sometimes they surprised Key and me, and sometimes they let us know the plans they were developing. Nothing ever happened like this, a secret from my mother, even if she was dead.

"Why doesn't Mom know?" I said.

My father looked like I'd hit him in the mouth. "I don't understand, little man."

I didn't trust any of this. "You do these things to-gether. Mom always knows. Why keep it from her?"

"Rad?" Key touched my hand. "Let Dad tell us his idea."

"That's right, Rad. Let me talk, okay? Let me tell you."

"But why doesn't Mom know?"

My father lost his patience.

"Konrad." He snarled my name. "Mom isn't here."

Key squeezed my hand. "So tell us," he said. "I want to know."

"I've planned a trip around the world by sailboat. I'm going to sell the house, buy a boat. I'll buy sailing lessons for all of us to start in August. Lessons in Mexico, the Sea of Cortes. And then we'll sail for a year or two years or for the rest of our lives. You won't go to school at all but you'll study, study, study like always, and you'll live, see the world, all the world's islands, and —"

"Sell the house?" I didn't believe a word of this. "Who'll buy it —? Oh, that's why you're fixing it up. You're going to go from doing nothing, ever, to doing everything, selling everything, and take us on a boat. Why don't you talk about this with Mom? Why don't you ask her? You just have to open your mouth and —"

My father had been sitting on a couch, but he stood up to his full height. "Stop talking." He clenched his fists.

"You —"

My father leaned down, his face a couple inches from mine. "Are you going to throw a tantrum, Rad? Are you going to lose your little mind?"

My father had my attention.

Key had disappeared. My father and I were the only two people on earth. And we were islands.

"You're weak," he went on. "You're out of control, just like my uncle, and you're untrustworthy."

"*I'm* untrustworthy?"

I might have shouted it.

My father raised his fists level to my chest, and I said nothing. Here is an example of a time when two instincts fought each other inside of me, the instinct to fight and the instinct to run.

"Get ahold of yourself." My father spoke through his teeth. "I will sell everything when I'm ready. And then we will sail around the world."

Anger, fear, shame, frustration, helplessness, sadness, suspicion, hatred: all these emotions running crazy through my head and heart.

I started to shake. Uncontrollably. My whole body.

"Well, at least you're not pissing down your legs." My father straightened up again. "Keep silent, little man. And get ahold of yourself."

Then he left.

And what did I do? I punched a wall and kicked the couch.

"Rad?" Key had reappeared behind me, and I spun on him.

"Don't —!" He raised his hands, hid his face, protecting himself.

I had, I admit, pulled back my fist as if —

"I would never hit you." I threw myself into the couch. "I would never. I just didn't know you were here anymore."

"I don't care." He crossed his arms and stared down at me.

I suddenly felt tired, and I waited.

Key just stood there, silent.

"Go ahead," I said finally. "Say what you want."

"We're going sailing around the world." It came out as a whisper.

"No," I said. "We're not."

■

I'm trying to get us to a moment, a very small fragment in a whole lifetime, the time it took for my father to punch out every window he could find, destroy furniture and cabinets and walls, a one-man wrecker, and nearly bleed to death, all of it taking less than ten minutes start to finish.

Like so much else, it's difficult to get the circumstances right. Honestly, I don't think any of us can have a pure memory of anything terrible or wonderful. The terribleness or wonderfulness itself warps us, twists around thought, perceptions, sensations. The whole experience, bad or good, has doubt sewn right through it. Was that thunderstorm really as scary as we thought? Was that movie really so funny?

As for the violence that came a couple nights after my father revealed his plan to sell the house and whatever else to sail around the world, I can only tell you the truth as I understand it.

My father made a dinner, a big and beautiful dinner. A slab of baked salmon with sprigs of dill and sliced lemon. Asparagus spears. Rice with herbs. I didn't even know he could cook like that, more than hot dogs.

Eleven days had gone by with him back in our lives. He was celebrating. And he came to the table without a hint of anything rough going on inside of him, only what seemed his good humor. This resembled, I thought later, the good humor he had for a little while years earlier when I wet myself at the dining-room table, when he came home drunk from the office and a fist fight, when he abdicated.

At this dinner with just Key and me, he smiled and hummed, he passed this bowl and that dish. All was peaceful. Until again, just like a few years before, with the model for me and the Barbie for my brother, he presented a gift.

Before ice cream and apple pie, after Key and I cleared the dishes, my father asked us to sit. He took two flat packages wrapped in brown paper from beside his chair and set them on the table.

"I have an announcement," my father said. "First, though, these gifts for my wife."

Wait.

Key looked over at me, unsure.

I understood. Not even I had noticed my ghost mother sitting with us.

"What's this, John?" If my dead mother felt at all nervous, she hid it well.

"Open the small one first."

My mother slid off the baker's string, red and white, binding the smaller of the two packages, and before she unfolded the butcher paper, she paused.

"Thank you," she said and smiled at my father.

"Don't thank me yet," my father said.

"I'm excited, that's all." And she uncovered the gift.

Drawings. My father's art.

The drawings.

Thirteen portraits, each one uglier and more

grotesque than the last, variations on a single theme: my mother asleep.

Sleeping: my mother's face like an ancient corpse, a mummy unwrapped, or a woman lifted out of a bog after forty centuries.

Sleeping: my mother's mouth distorted by a dream, her eyes partially open, rolled up under the half-closed lids, eerie, the whites of her eyes and two slender arcs of her irises revealed.

Sleeping: my mother's hand under her chin, blunt fingernails, prominent veins, sharp knuckles, the ugly hands of a hairless monkey.

Sleeping: my mother's impossibly long throat exposed, her jaw, her long chin, her nostrils like a baboon's, her short eyelashes, the deep ridge of her brow.

Sleeping: my mother's uneven mouth, and her lips, the full lower lip and the thin upper lip, and a tooth exposed, a fang.

Sleeping: strands of my mother's hair covering her face, resembling a woman drowned, bloated, tangled in seaweed.

On and on. Thirteen times my mother asleep.

"You like them, darling?" My father and his voice had gone dangerously soft.

My mother sifted through the thirteen portraits. Her mouth a thin line.

"Nothing to say?" My father drilled into my mother with an expression of — I don't know what. Not hatred or anger. Maybe curiosity. As if he were showing his art to a critic he wanted to win over. "What do you think?"

"I don't know what to think." My mother stared at the drawing that looked as if she had drowned in her sleep. "I don't want to know what you were thinking."

All the drawings had been done in sepia, a sickly brown closer to red. For some reason I thought it might have been my father's blood and not ink. The blood, the ink, had long dried, but each of the portraits was a fresh and open wound.

"Go ahead," my father said, his voice black and brittle like charcoal. "Open the painting."

My mother shook her head.

"Open the package and then we can move on to more important things. My plans for all of us. I have plans, you know."

My mother shook her head. "No, John. I don't know what's happening, but —"

"Not another word, darling." The word *darling* was not an endearment but a curse. My father took back the second package. "I'll untie it for you."

And that's when my mother cracked wide open.

No.

That's when I cracked wide open.

At that moment, with my father's effort, a full dinner on top of everything else he'd done over the past eleven days, to insult my mother, my dead mother, to make her look ugly, to use these portraits for hate —

I dropped the portraits onto the table, and I threw myself at my father. I had a butter knife. I meant only to destroy the second package, the painting, with the knife. I didn't want to see it, didn't want it unwrapped by anyone. I was all elbows and fists, armed with an almost harmless knife, but I managed to knock the package out of my father's hand and somehow landed my fists on his face and cut open his ear. Blood enough for a drawing, maybe, a small drawing of a kiwi or the head of a squirrel.

My father shot up out of his chair and grabbed my hands. He pulled me right across the end of the table and forced me down onto the floor in front of him.

The knife clattered out of reach. I cried out.

My father growled, raised his fist. "I will absolutely —"

He might have finished his thought, but Key had moved. Twelve, not especially big, not especially strong, not especially fast, more clumsy than nimble, but my brother had moved.

He shoved my father hard, forcing him to let go of me.

My father punched wildly and connected once, somewhere soft. My father swung again. He swung, and I felt my head break, my jaw come unhinged, my cheek split.

"Stop, please." Key began his screaming. My calm, peaceful brother came apart. "Stop. Daddy, stop."

I was lying on the floor, my head filled with a hundred trains, and my brother scrambled toward me.

My father turned away from me, roaring, and in his fury he found a purpose: to destroy the house.

My father became a cannon, blowing out the windows one after another with five-pound fists, kicking in cabinets and breaking walls with ten-pound boots, like round shot. He shouted and grunted and cursed, punched and punched and punched, kicked and kicked. Shattering cabinet doors, glass, drywall, wood.

My mother covered me with her body. She lay on top of me as if to protect me against a tornado and its spiraling debris, or a bomb blast, splinters of glass, wood, plaster, bone, flying nails, all of it sharp enough to slice anyone to threads.

"I know you're hurt," my mother whispered into my ear, "but keep your face to the floor."

I wanted to ask her a question, but I couldn't move my mouth properly. The trains, speeding and tumbling along their steel tracks.

"We'll get through this. Your father won't kill you and Key."

I wasn't so sure.

Everything stopped. Silence.

A few moments, questioning the quiet.

My brother was crying, sitting in a ball, his hands over his ears. But my father?

My mother crawled off me. "Wait here. Don't move."

I couldn't move even if I had wanted to. I passed out.

As Key explained later, he crawled toward the doorway between the dining room and living room, altogether unsure where my father had gone. The front door was open. My father had left. He'd left bleeding. He trailed blood out into the yard, enough blood for a thousand drawings of my mother asleep, a path of blood across the grass to the already ancient Subaru, the car my father bought after selling the SUV and sports car from his family and lawyering days. He drove off, out of the cul-de-sac.

My brother, his face a wreck with grief and fear and a little egg forming over his eye — From what? My father's fist? — came back and sat by me. He was trembling. I was sitting up, bruised and concussed, my head lolling against Key's shoulder.

My jaw was painful, but I could speak. "Where'd he go?"

"The hospital, I hope."

"Do you see her?"

"Who?"

"Mom."

"Mom?"

My mother headed toward the kitchen. Glass, wood, rubble crunching under her feet.

"No," Key said. "I don't ever see her."

I can tell you, this was one of the few times in my life when I felt nothing at all. No fear, no anger, no sadness. All my emotion had dried up. I was calm. My jaw and my head were exploding, but my heart? Numb.

SIX

We're surrounded by maps. Maps everywhere, in everything. In the faces of everyone around us. All people wear a map of one kind or another.

Some maps can't be trusted. You set out, and without warning you're lost. You think you're in one place only to find out you're nowhere at all, nowhere recognizable.

My father's face had a map like this. You might have thought you could know the man from his map. He had a dimple in his chin, dimples in his cheeks, a dimple just left of center in his forehead, a scar from chicken pox. These four little dents made a skewed diamond if you connected them, which now makes sense. He looked friendly, even goofy. He looked trustworthy. He had a map of good nature in his face, but his face was, instead, a map of the far side of the moon.

Maps change as we get to know the world. The smarter we get, the more we learn. Maps go from rough to refined, from inaccurate to accurate. Look at early, early maps of the world, of the whole planet, its continents and oceans and seas as people imagined them. Early maps of India or Africa or Asia. Or the Americas, especially Canada and the North, before these places were known and charted. The continents in ancient maps belong to a planet other than earth. They are unrecognizable and almost laughable.

The map of Jacqui's face was this kind of map. I saw her first at twelve, and she was so totally new and unexplored, nothing like anyone else, something more fantastic and frightening and exciting and good. And when I got to know her, she lost her mysterious frontier. She became a map redrawn. I could navigate her, and I could chart her. Her map changed. It became more accurate. It was accurate until the land between us changed, until she chose someone else over me, until our world broke apart. And then I had to abandon everything I knew. I ended up for a long while without a map.

Maps change. Some islands may be lost to the ocean. Weather and tides eat up the shoreline, gobbling land, changing geometry and geography. Volcanic eruptions, earthquakes, meteorites. Blazing missiles from space. Cataclysms change the shape of land, can kill the land. My mother's face was a map of youth until it became a map of heartache and tiredness, a map of pain. Then she became a map of death.

You can trust some maps to tell you everything you need to know. You know me when you see me. I'm a map of the Sahara, impassable and inhospitable and uninhabitable. You can visit, but you can't stay.

Some maps are maps of the imagination. Maps of places that exist only in the mind of the mapmaker. What's the map of Atlantis? Or the island of Robinson Crusoe or Azkaban? What's the true and accepted map of my brother, Key?

Nothing about Key seems beyond doubt or argument. Not even his eyes. I say they're green, but? Or his hair, brown or black? We're twins, but some people question whether we're related at all. We're more complementary than alike. His expression seems to belong to a girl, a boy, and sometimes to a peaceful and rare animal or a sprite. Barely human. In a good way.

I don't know. People see what they want or need in Key's face. He's real enough, he has a voice and a body and a mind. He walks around, gets good grades. But there's nothing to say for sure he isn't also made up.

■

A few months ago, Key told me he'd mastered circular breathing. When he wants, he can inhale as he exhales. It's not that exactly. There are subtleties.

Since ancient days, circular breathing has been practiced in meditation, crafts, and music. Yogis, glassblowers, swordsmiths, and players of the trumpet, bagpipes, and didgeridoo. A man using circular breathing, my brother told me, once held the same note on a saxophone for the better part of an hour. That was good enough for the world record.

Key isn't always circular breathing, but he practices it, meditates with it three or four times a day. He told me it brings him peace. He told me he can recite a prayer or a question or a koan without stopping so that the spirit of what he says takes him over from the inside.

"Is this to get over Harrison?"

"It's more than that."

"What kind of questions or prayers? Like, What's the sound of one hand clapping?"

"I don't think you understand. I want to repeat something simple as often as I can without stopping, repeat it no matter what I'm doing, where I am. Doing this can build my confidence and my faith and my heart."

"What *is* the sound of one hand clapping, though?"

Key looked at me and reached out his hand.

What was I supposed to do? Take it? Not take it?

"The sound of one hand clapping could be silence," Key said. "Or it could be a hand in midair waiting for another hand, or a hand in midair waiting to do something meaningful."

I realize now, Key knew more about being a monk than I ever will. He knows more about prayer and God and patience.

"You mentioned prayers, Key. You said you want to say these things over and over to build your faith and heart. Faith in what?"

"I want to be love."

Wow, I thought, *everything we've been through has come to this. My brother is the one who's crazy.*

"I can see what you're thinking, Rad. I'm not crazy. If I want to, I can become love."

"No one can *be* love," I said.

"I can. I can say to myself over and over, *I am love*, and saying it enough will make it true. It might take a long time, but —"

"So, if I say enough times that I'm a walrus —"

"Hilarious," Key said, unimpressed. "I think you could be walrus-like if you convince yourself of it. If you say it enough times. But what's a walrus anyway?"

I stared at him, wondering for the millionth time in our lives what he could possibly be saying to me.

"Do you believe me, Rad, that I could be love?"

"Yes." I knew he could be love, if being love was anything like being a lawyer or a heart surgeon or a painter. "Yes, Key. You want to be love? Sure, go ahead. But what does that mean any more than being a walrus?"

"I don't know, actually. I'm not saying I could be love right now. I don't think I'm old enough. I don't think I have the discipline. I get hurt too easily. I get sad, and I get happy, and I worry. Love doesn't own any of these things for itself."

"So you're practicing to be love?" Did I ask this, for real? Yes, I asked it, and I was serious. "You can use the circular breathing to say *I am love* over and over, all day, waking to sleeping, 24/7?"

"Yes. At some point I'll be able to say *I am love* with every breath, in and out, and this will make it true."

"How old will you have to be to be love?"

"I don't know," he said. "At least twenty."

■

An hour after I found my brother on the platform and my father dead, an hour after I carried him into the house, twenty minutes after I broke a pitcher of water in my rage while we sat in the kitchen among the ghosts of our father, I remembered this conversation with Key about becoming love.

Key and I had been talking about what happened with my father. He'd told me a dream had descended on them, come down over them, and then my father had fallen away.

"You once told me about becoming love," I said. "Remember?"

"Yes. It wasn't that long ago. So?"

"Were you practicing becoming love while you were on the platform with Dad?"

Key made no sound or move.

"Key? Were you standing there with our father, breathing circularly, meditating in a dream with him, becoming love or something?"

"I don't know. Maybe."

"What do you mean by love, anyway?"

"It's about compassion and sympathy and kindness. Not romance or sex."

"Okay, Key. I'm trying to understand what you were doing with Dad. You were there with compassion and sympathy, right?"

Key started rocking again, shaking.

"I just want to know what happened. I mean, the other night was weird. More than weird. The night Dad attacked you."

"He hugged me at first on the platform, like I said."

"I'm not accusing you of anything, Key." My fists, stones, heavy in my lap. "That's not what I'm doing."

"Dad loved me," Key said. "He loved you. But he really loved Mom."

"I know. I'm just trying to understand your dream and how Dad came to fall."

"I went to Dad. I wasn't there very long. He wasn't making much sense, talking about Mom. Then he hugged me. He was looking wild and then, maybe, fragile. You know he couldn't be trusted anymore. I wanted him to stay calm. I wanted to figure out how to get him up the ladder, off the platform."

"And so you were peaceful and loving, and then what?"

"I don't know, Rad. I told you we were in a dream. And then —"

"You told me you didn't know if you'd pushed him."

"Why are you doing this? Why are you asking me these questions?"

"I'm —"

"A dream and then —"

"I know." I stood, my fists on the table between us. "I know, I know. And then Dad was falling. I'm confused, Key. I'm worried."

"Are you angry with me, Konrad? Angry with everything you can't understand? Angry because life, your heart and mind, are always out of your control? Because you can't trust yourself?"

Key was not yet love, at least not all the time. I'm the person Key hurts when he's upset. I'm the person who will take his pain when he gives it to me.

And just then, the map of his face was the map of fear and his own confusion. I felt my own heart drop and my fists rise up.

"Are you going to hit me? Or are you going to hit something else?"

"Is that what you want?"

"Smashing the pitcher not enough?" Key started to lose himself. "Sometimes I wish I were you, Rad. You can do and say anything because everyone knows you're half-crazy."

"Yeah, it's super fun."

"No, I'm sure it's terrible. But at least you can feel it and let it all go. You might have to pay for it —"

"I'll die young, right?"

"I'm sorry I said that. I'm only trying to say you get to live freely. That's your privilege."

So the people with rough minds are free? Maybe. Sort of. But that's a freedom just about all of us would give up. Chaos isn't the same thing as freedom. Lack of order isn't the same thing as freedom.

Freedom, whether we like it or not, is organized. Freedom isn't anarchy.

I wish I had said something like this to Key. Instead, I proved my brother right.

I hammered my fists on the table. I hammered and I hammered.

And then I crossed the kitchen and punched the refrigerator, denting it.

"Look at you now, Rad." Key was on his feet, shouting. "Look at you. Why are you allowed to do this? Why are you hitting things?"

■

Why am I hitting things? Because I want to.

I'm free.

See this? This is freedom, right?

I will hit the wall. I will hit myself.

I want to.

And you want to know what it's like in my head right now? You want to know?

It's like this:

... ! @ # $ % ^ & *)
(*&^%$#@@#$%^&*&^%!@#$%^&*)(*&^*!@#
$%*&^%!*!@#$%^&!@!*&^%#$^%$#@!%^&*&
^%$#@!@#$%&^^%$!!!@#$%^&^%$*&^%$#!)
(@#$%$#@#$%^&!*...

And this:

...hammerfisthammerfisthammerfistsawfist-
toothhammerpliersfistboneclubfisthammerpliers-
sawtongsfistsawhammertoothbonespikenailnailnail-
spikehammertoothbonesawclubknife...

And:

It gets harder to live outside. It gets harder to live inside.

And then, at last, this:

>emptiness<

Sadness.

SEVEN

Five years ago, my father tore open Key and me at the dinner table and nearly bled to death in his car. He survived his injuries, and my brother and I survived ours.

My brother had a black eye. We both had long hair that fell over our faces, and Key might have hidden his bruised and swollen eye except he decided to shave his head. Twelve years old and his auburn fuzz, his freckles, and bright eyes — for a month he looked sort of like a copper elf. If anything, after this event, my brother grew quieter, calmer, gentler. He smiled and smiled. Not a broad, the-world's-my-oyster smile, but a slight smile, a Mona Lisa smile, as if he were listening to the music of the spheres, music only he could hear, or to the running monologue of an actor not quite funny enough to make him laugh out loud.

And me? My face, bruised and scraped when my father drove me head first into the floor next to his chair, healed. I think my father knocked my jaw out of line. It might click forever when I chew. Maybe one day I'll have my jaw reset, fixed surgically. I'll do it if only to get rid of the headaches. But let's be honest. It's hard to imagine the monks of Lérins paying for my comfort when their God asks me to suffer.

I'm just guessing.

As for my father, he survived his deep cuts from smashing wood and glass, but he had destroyed what was left of his family and practically destroyed his house. He wouldn't fix it up to sell. We would never learn to sail or leave on a boat to circumnavigate the world. My father never again made us a dinner. He disappeared inside himself. At last.

Poof.

■

Key and I cleaned up the wreckage of our kitchen, cleared the dust and rubble and glass. We covered the windows with cardboard and plastic sheeting to keep out the weather and wind. This cut back the amount of light into the kitchen. The house seemed even sadder. Dark. Meanwhile, the doors came off all the cabinets, and we covered the holes in the walls with plastic. That's the best we could do.

My father never spoke to us, and he seemed all but gone. We didn't know what he was doing day to day. He might have disappeared for days at a time, maybe left the house, or simply hid from us, out of our sight. Key and I occasionally found a can or carton in the garbage, apple cores and avocado rinds, proof of life.

Once we accepted our father's absence, life got easier, even with the house a shambles. We could breathe. Like a flat one-ton stone had been lifted off our chests.

Three months after that dinner that ended in blood, Key was riding a bus and happened to spot our father walking into a supermarket.

"He looked terrible, Rad. Skinny, like he hasn't eaten more than walnuts and apples and avocados since that night."

I tapped my jaw. "I don't care if he starves to death."

"You don't mean that."

Sometimes I don't understand Key at all.

"Of course I mean it," I said. "I wouldn't give him a crumb if it would save him."

Silence.

Then, "Walnuts and apples, Key?"

"I don't know. Small things. Not enough to live on."

"We can only hope."

Key shook his head. "Don't say that."

"Do you forgive him?"

"I don't think I can."

"Well, I can't either," I said.

"We're not talking about the same thing, Rad. You're too angry to forgive him. You don't think he deserves forgiveness. I'm saying I can't forgive him because I don't understand what happened. And I don't think it's up to me to forgive him. That's for Dad to do or not."

"Forgive himself? Why just him? Why not us, too?"

"You're asking why we shouldn't also be allowed to forgive him?"

I clenched my fists. "I don't know. You've gotten me confused."

"Don't get upset, Rad. I'm not trying to trip you up. I'm saying it's Dad's choice to forgive Dad or not."

"Why?"

"Whatever happened, happened inside of Dad. We don't know anything about it."

I honestly couldn't even pretend to understand what Key was saying. We have two different kinds of intelligence.

"Are you saying Dad might still love us? That he might get back to us again? Even now?"

"It's not impossible."

My head was spinning. "Do you love Dad?"

Key thought for a moment. "I love the Dad I knew first, the Dad that came with Mom. I don't know the John Schoe that —"

"I don't think we have to do anything for Dad," I said. "We don't owe him anything. We don't have to forgive him. We don't have to understand him. He has to know what he did was wrong. He's done nothing for us. Nothing except hurt us."

Key watched my face for a long time.

"We have to keep helping ourselves," I said.

"You're right," Key said. But he was thinking of something else.

"What?" I said.

"He's sick."

"Sick?"

"Dad's going insane."

My brother went to the living room couch and wrapped himself up in a blanket. I followed him.

"Insane? Like something's changed him? A tumor? Cancer?"

"No," Key said. "I mean like his uncle. The one who lived in the hospital. Dad told us, remember? His biggest fear."

I sat down on the couch next to my brother. I wondered if this changed everything, everything that ever happened.

If Dad was sick, losing his mind, when did it start? It could have started a long time ago, long before Mom died, maybe even before he gave up his job. Maybe he's always been —

"Crazy," I said.

Key nodded. "And no one can do anything about it."

"But there are psychiatrists. Doctors. Drugs. I mean, he didn't have to give up."

Key was quiet.

"I'm scared," he said finally.

■

What is it about islands? Their strangeness and isolation, reachable only by boat or by swimming, or, I guess, in some places by sled or skis.

We think about the castaway on a deserted island. We have an image of a tiny island with a palm tree. We think of beautiful vacations on islands. We think of the miraculous worlds that can be built on islands, like Manhattan and Abu Dhabi.

There's something very strange about the fact that islands can interrupt oceans. Even tiny islands, uninhabitable or hostile islands, have their own geography and sometimes their own weather.

Islands are fragments. They're pieces broken off from larger pieces, the smithereens and fractions of continents. They've floated off, some farther than others.

And there are islands spat out by volcanoes. They're fragments, too, proof of lava, proof of the earth's interior rage and violence.

I wish I could spit out islands, burning islands, islands that cool down after a long time and then support life. Islands with black sand and hot springs, like Iceland. I wish my emotions could give birth to something beautiful. Something that could support palm trees and monkeys and toucans.

Whole civilizations have imagined themselves as islands, whether they lived on actual islands or not. They imagined themselves surrounded by oceans of land, oceans of mountains or prairies or sand or forest or ice, surrounded by oceans of barbarians, foreigners, people not exactly like them, but not exactly different either. We've never really wanted to accept that humanity is one continent. We can't do it. We don't really know how to be a part of a whole. We make ourselves into islands. Always, one way or another, we break away and float off.

We're lonely, whether we know it or not, but we don't have to be. We could choose to rebuild the continent.

We could, but we won't.

∎

I've thought about becoming a cartographer, but almost all mapmaking happens now through computer programming, sorting through information from satellites and GPS. I hate technology. Unfortunately, I also hate to draw. I don't think I've ever held a pencil or crayon or brush and not felt angry. I'm more like a gorilla with a pointed stick than a human holding a pencil. I'd do better rooting and scraping for insects in tree bark than drawing or writing. I can only read maps. I can only study.

Six hundred years ago, in 1420, a man named Cristoforo Buondelmonti published the first *Liber insularum*, or book of islands. His *Liber insularum Archipelagi*, a book of the insular, from the Latin *insularium*, contained maps with descriptions of the

Greek islands and archipelagos, the islands and archipelagos of the Aegean and Ionian seas. He included some of the important far eastern Mediterranean cities like Constantinople, now Istanbul, and historically significant places such as Gallipoli. Buondelmonti was an Italian from Florence and a monk — a monk! — and it's possible he compiled his new kind of book on Rhodes, a Greek island closer to the Turkish coast eleven miles north than to mainland Athens 267 miles north-northwest.

I'm about to go a little off course. I can feel it. This bridge I'm building is growing an arm.

I hope you like history.

Rhodes is an island famous for one of the Seven Wonders of the Ancient World, the Colossus, a giant statue of iron and marble, sheathed in bronze, representing the Greek titan-god of the Sun, Helios. It stood only fifty-some years before falling in an earthquake.

Rhodes is an island for tourists, an island of spas and ruins. It's where you'd find the Palace of the Grand Master, the castle and fortifications once occupied by the Knights of Rhodes, also known as the Knights of St. John of Jerusalem, or the Knights Hospitaller. An ancient religious order founded around the year 1020, the Hospitallers had for almost three hundred years offered care and then armed support to Christian pilgrims traveling to the Holy Land. The

Hospitallers abandoned the Holy Land after the fall of the Kingdom of Jerusalem to the forces of the Sultan of Egypt in 1291.

They found a home on an island, Cyprus, an island at this moment contested and divided between Turkey and Greece. Once the politics, even then, got too hot, the Hospitallers left Cyprus, taking over Rhodes and a few other islands in 1309. The Hospitallers rebranded themselves the Knights of Rhodes and remained there for two centuries.

Buondelmonti, the traveling monk and cartographer, might have drawn up his book of maps while a guest of the famous Catholic order. He arrived in the middle of the Knights' occupation of Rhodes, a century after they took over the island and turned it into a fortress. The Knights thought a smallish island would be easy to defend. And they kept their island against waves of Barbary pirates and two Ottoman invasions before they finally lost in 1522 to a third Ottoman invasion, to the Emperor Suleiman the Magnificent and his giant army. So Buondelmonti created his maps of the Grecian islands, his *liber insularum*, on an island stronghold held by an armed and very powerful religious order.

And where did the Knights of Rhodes, the Hospitallers, go after 1522 when Suleiman conquered the island?

They wandered, more or less, until 1530, when Charles I of Spain, also King of Sicily (the largest island in the Mediterranean, off the toe of the Italian boot), gave the Knights another island: Malta. The Knights of Rhodes, once the Knights of St. John of Jerusalem, rebranded themselves again, this time as the Knights of Malta. During their time on Malta, in the middle of the seventeenth century, the Knights actually came to possess four islands in the Caribbean, not too far from Puerto Rico — St. Barthélemy, St. Christopher, St. Martin, and St. Croix — which they turned around and sold in 1665 to the French West India Company. The Knights held on to Malta for another 130 years.

Then, in 1799, five hundred years after the Knights Hospitaller fled the Egyptian sultan, abandoning the Holy Land, they got creamed by Napoleon. Napoleon, future self-proclaimed emperor of France. The same Napoleon who would crush most of Europe over twenty years. He was from the island of Corsica located in the Tyrrhenian Sea, off the coasts of Italy and France, and he was twice exiled to islands — to Elba, just off the coast of northern Italy (a bad choice, since he escaped and returned to power only to lose everything at the Battle of Waterloo to another great island general, England's Duke of Wellington), and then to St. Helena, a tiny, rocky speck in the southern

Atlantic (a good choice, since he died there). Napoleon conquered the Knights on his way to ... Egypt. Phew.

Hang with me a little longer about this Knights business.

In 1806, a little unbelievably, or maybe not so much, the Knights of Malta, once the Knights of Rhodes, once the Knights Hospitaller, also known as the Knights of St. John of Jerusalem, were offered — that's right — another island. This time, the Swedes suggested the Knights take up residence on their largest island, Gotland, sitting off their eastern coast, out in the Baltic Sea.

The Knights refused. They'd had enough of islands. And they missed Malta. Who wouldn't? The weather's beautiful.

∎

And what about the Florentine monk, Buondelmonti? He started a tradition of European mapmaking — island cartography, maps of the insular — that lasted two hundred years. A genre of maps and atlases that lasted deep into the European age of discovery — into the age of colonization; into the rise of the first age of globalization, of worldwide commerce; the long age of slavery; the rise of genocide and the deep hatreds everyone everywhere is trying to survive right now — when Portugal, Spain, Italy, and France, when England and Holland and Germany and Sweden and Denmark, all of them, all of them, sailed the world and took it over. The rise of European empires.

Just like love, beauty takes some space for itself in the history of knowledge and ugliness. I'm not sure anyone could look at the maps created in the cartographic workshops of the European countries that took over and carved up the world, the workshops where cartographers labored with ink and compasses and rulers and dividers, and not say the maps are shockingly beautiful. They had their calligraphy, their gold leaf and their inlay, their mysteries, all their art and science, and they were the property of kingdoms, kingdoms that would put down a hundred million roads, through land and water to all kinds of heavens and hells.

And today, the maps and atlases from this era can auction to collectors for hundreds of thousands, even millions of dollars.

The most beautiful map I have ever seen may not be the most beautiful map to anyone else. It's an undated and anonymous map of the eastern Mediterranean, like Buondelmonti's, but a portolan, a kind of map used by captains and navigators to pilot their ships. A portolan has a hundred, two hundred fine straight lines crisscrossing the face of it, a web of wind roses. It's like looking at a map through a net. The lines pass through all the islands and peninsulas painted in blue and yellow and red and green, through the distant author's indecipherable writing, his names for the parts of the sea, the harbors, the bays and headlands.

The lines lead you everywhere and nowhere. This is a map, really, of a human being, a human brain: beautiful, complicated, starting and ending over and over, and almost totally unknowable.

EIGHT

Time goes fast when you have to think about surviving. Years flew.

Around the middle of ninth grade, a couple of years after his great violence at the dinner table, our father started to come out of his room, the room that had been his bedroom with our mother. He let himself be seen. Useless, vacant, he drifted between rooms, sometimes sitting for hours at a time, or standing here and there.

He had long before stopped supplying us with money. My brother and I had worked for cash — yard work, odd jobs, babysitting — before we turned fourteen, when we could get real work. We worked fast food. We're both managers now, the youngest in the chain. We've sometimes talked about opening up a restaurant of our own, or a food truck. But that would get in the way of Key's Ivy League future and my monastic life.

The house had slid backwards, decaying at a faster rate. Key and I used our salaries to repair the house a little. We used the same book of home repair my father had used to fix the roof. We bought windows and replaced the broken ones in the kitchen. We gave ourselves the gift of light.

Key and I learned how to repair the walls my father had broken through. And, almost three years after our father lost his mind, we had a functional kitchen again. Not pretty, but functional.

Our father wandered around. He would sometimes watch us work, putting up drywall, glazing the new windows, and from time to time he'd greet us when he saw us. But then he'd disappear again, travel over some body of water to his island, someplace separate. Whatever ailed him made him almost un-reachable. That's the truth. It made him an uncharted island.

Every so often, our father would appear in some part of the house, almost ghostly, silent and station-ary, just as he did when I wanted to kill myself after Jacqui slept with some guy at debate camp. Key and I didn't need him for anything, but he was there, a presence.

Sometimes he'd try and make small talk about the weather, or ask after us, how we slept, how school was going. The exchanges could get weird fast.

"So, Rad, what's happening?" His eyes would seem unfocused, almost as if he'd been staring for hours through a telescope at the stars a billion miles off and couldn't see clearly anything within arm's reach.

"Not much. You?"

"Oh, I don't know. I thought I was hungry, but I'm not. Are you hungry?"

"No, I'm not hungry."

"I thought about catching eels. Have you ever eaten an eel?"

"Not yet."

"I'm not sure I want to skin an eel, to be honest."

"No one will force you to skin an eel, Dad."

"I'm pretty sure you have to skin an eel before you eat it. The skin carries the electricity, and if you bite into an eel that hasn't been skinned, that hasn't had the electricity taken out of it, you'll get the shock of your life. Your whole mouth full of lightning."

"I'm not sure that's true, Dad."

"True or not, I think it's better not to catch and skin eels."

The End.

He simply slid away to some other room in the house.

Our father never mentioned our mother, and he never mentioned what happened the night he attacked Key and me and bled a river.

Then, one afternoon fourteen months ago, our father disappeared. Or so Key and I thought. There were times when he'd gone for a walk and called the home phone when he didn't recognize where he'd ended up. One of us would have to bring him home.

For some reason, though, on this afternoon, Key and I felt more afraid than usual when we didn't find our father at home. We *felt* he had disappeared, that he hadn't just gone to his interior island but had left for good.

The garage was open — this was before my brother sealed it shut — but no sign of our father.

"Oh, Rad," Key said. He took off toward the basement.

"Wait, what?"

"The ravine."

We decided without saying anything that our father had fallen to his death.

And I'll confess right here, now, I couldn't tell whether or not I wanted him to be lying at the bottom of the ravine. All the sudden horror, and all the sudden freedom, rushing at Key and me at the same time.

Maybe it *would* be better if —

We found our father out back. Wood, hammer, nails, a shovel, spade. He had cleared the ferns that once carpeted the ground past the stilts that held up our deck. He was lying on his stomach, working the dirt, digging, scraping.

"Dad?" Key walked over to him. "Hello?"

Our father looked over his shoulder, calm and alert. "Key, hi."

"Everything okay?"

"Good, yes." He sat up. "How're you doing, Rad?"

I shrugged. I was still trying to calm myself.

Question: Was I relieved or disappointed?

Answer: Yes.

Key said, "What are you doing there, Dad?"

My father looked around, smiling. "I'm going to build a ladder down the wall of the ravine."

"All the way to the bottom?"

"No, of course not. I'm going to build a platform. I want to sit among the trees and stones."

Key and I looked at each other.

"By yourself?" Key said. "Dad, you could die."

"I won't die," he laughed. "I'll do what I can by myself. You'll help if I need it, I know you will. But I don't think I'll need the help."

Key and I more or less stood there staring at him.

"I can do this," our father said, smiling up at us.

"How?" I said. "How can you do this without falling?"

"My secret," he said, the smile gone. "Now run along, you two. I'm fine."

Key and I said nothing, both of us wondering if by walking away we would be giving up on him.

"Please," our father said. "I can do this. Look, I'm checking the ground and the cliff, seeing how they're made, checking the rock ledge. Then I'm going to build the ladder up here in the garage, a ladder of slats and steel cord. Something collapsible, but with a little structure. I'll anchor it in the stone and tie it off to the house. Then I'll anchor it here and there as I go down."

"Are you serious?" Me again.

"And I'll make the platform in pieces. Interlocking, you know?" My father ignored me, watching his vision instead, watching himself descend his ladder into the ravine. "Steel and wood, a big sturdy puzzle, cantilevered, and —. Well, I haven't figured everything out yet. But I will."

"Dad," Key began. "Can't you just sit on the back porch? You're not a carpenter, let alone —"

"I know what I'm doing, boys. And now it's time for you to leave me alone."

We stood there not quite sure what to do.

"I said move along." His voice had turned black. "Don't make me stand up, okay?"

I was bigger than my father by then, and I knew I could defend the two of us against him, but I tugged Key away by the sleeve.

Before we went in through the basement door, we looked back at him, at our father of sorts, as he worked from his belly, chipping, digging, scraping.

■

My ghost mother had no idea what to do or say that night when I told her about my father's project. Would she have me lock him out of the garage? Sell off his tools?

"Promise me you'll at least talk to him, Rad. For me."

I promised.

And when I went to him, he said, lucid and strong, "I've already talked to your mom. I told her I won't die.

I'm focused. I know I can do this." He tapped the side of his head and frowned. "I need this, understand?"

"Yeah, I understand," I said. "But do you understand it's frightening? You understand we don't want you to do this? Even if Mom —"

"Yes."

And, for the first time, my dead mother appeared to my father without appearing to me. She must have, because my father said, "That's not fair, Diane."

A moment when my mother must have been talking to him.

My father sighed, half-growled. "I'm not me, Diane. Or fully me. I know that. I've got one ending ahead of me, and it's not the ending I want."

Key appeared next to me, home from work.

"What's going on?" he whispered, but I shook my head.

We watched my father talk with our mother.

"I'm saying I want to leave the planet long before you or the boys have to see me or deal with me at my worst. I don't want you or Key or Rad to deal with any of it. And I don't want to go to a hospital."

"Any of what?" That's what my mother must have said.

"The dirty work of whatever this is. Losing what's left of my mind. My long death."

"That's not your decision."

"Yes, it is." And with that, my father stood up. "You can let me stay here, Diane, let me build the ladder and platform, let me be alive here for as long as I can bear it, around you, around the boys, the people I love, or you can let me go right now. I'll go this second. Step off that ledge into the great abyss."

My ghost mother might have been silent.

"Do we have an understanding?"

My father worked when he had his concentration and wits. It took him through the winter and into spring to put together his ladder of teak and steel cord and steel brackets. And he built his platform, eight interlocking pieces, just as he said. All of it, beginning to end, he did alone.

May, a year ago, after the spring rain had stopped, my father tied off his ladder to the stilts holding up the back porch and fastened his ladder into the ground where the ferns used to grow, then into the stone ledge, and let it down the wall of the ravine. With only a length of rope knotted around his waist and to one of the stilts, he assembled his cantilevered platform piece by piece, fastening it to brackets he'd embedded in the stone. He anchored two steel cords to the face of ravine and hooked them into thick eyes he'd screwed into the front of the platform. Two taut cables, two brackets, so the whole shebang had support from above and below.

Finally, the time came when Key and I had to watch our father carry a decrepit folding chair down to the platform. He went over the ledge on hands and knees, the chair hanging off his shoulder.

"Do you want me to bring the chair down, Dad?" Key had to volunteer, his care shining through, while I waited to see what would happen.

"No, thank you." Our father getting his bearings, positioning his hands and feet on the slats, shrugging the chair up further onto his back. "I got it."

Key and I waited. We expected a great cracking as the platform failed, pitching our father to his death. We expected a long scream as he fell to the bottom of the ravine.

Silence.

"Dad?" Key got to his belly and inched his way to the ledge. "Dad?"

A moment later, peering down over the edge, Key waved his hand for me to come forward.

"Seriously?"

I got down and crawled to the ledge.

There, almost twenty-five feet down, my father, sitting on his chair.

For the rest of his short life, he would go to his platform to sit. He'd gaze out from his island toward the horizon, across an ocean he'd invented.

■

Six months ago, I found my father lying on the floor of the kitchen. He was holding his head in his hands and writhing on the floor.

"Dad?"

"Help me."

"What can I do?"

"Get Diane. Get my wife. She'll know what I need."

I was helpless.

"Mom." I shouted it. If ever I wanted her to appear. "Mom."

Nothing, and my father started banging his head on the floor. "Make it stop. Make it stop."

I threw myself onto my father and held his head against my chest. I clamped him in my legs and arms, but he fought. He fought.

"Please. Where's Diane? She'll know."

Then he passed out. Maybe the pain knocked him out.

I sat there on the kitchen floor until I laid my father down on his side. I tried to make him as comfortable as possible, and I waited.

Fifteen minutes he slept. And then he reached for his head. He seemed to check his jaw and cheek, as if his head had broken or burst into pieces.

"Still hurting?"

My father nodded.

"A little better, though?"

"Yes."

"Can I get you anything?"

"Water."

I poured my father a glass of water from the pitcher I would break months later. He drank it slowly.

"What happened?" I said.

"Headache."

I'd never known my father to have headaches, migraines. I get headaches, especially when I get upset, but —

"Migraine?"

My father lowered his glass and shook his head.

"What would you call it then?"

"Something else. It's everything in my head trying to break out."

"Is this the first one?"

"No."

"How long, then? When did they start?"

"I don't know. A year ago? They've gotten worse."

"You don't think you should go to a doctor?"

My father shook his head. "I can't seem to get my wife to make the call, and I'm not sure she wants me to go at all. What can a doctor do anyway?"

"I don't know," I started. "MRI? Painkillers?" I could hear my own sarcasm, and I didn't much like it. I tried to soften my tone. "Maybe it's something we should know about. A tumor or something?"

My father looked at me out of the corner of his eye. "Can you turn off the light?"

I turned it off.

I said, "You want to stand up and go somewhere else to lie down?"

"No. I'm fine here. I'm waiting for my wife."

I looked around for my mother.

Mom? Nothing.

My father closed his eyes, rubbed his head. "I'm sorry you had to see that."

"How much does it hurt now?"

"Nothing like it did, but it still might knock down a horse."

"That's bad. Can I take you to a doctor? Call an ambulance?"

"That's up to my wife. Do you know Diane?"

I closed my own eyes and rubbed my temples.

"I know her," I said.

"She's something, right?"

"Something else," I agreed.

My father looked at me from half-closed eyes. His eyes looked black and hollow.

"If you don't mind my asking," he said, "who are you?"

■

You can ask, why didn't I — why didn't we — get my father help? He might have had a tumor or some terrible illness. Like Alzheimer's. There were the headaches that tore him open. The forgetfulness, the hallucinations.

This is how the conversation went between Key and me after that first time I witnessed my father's pain.

Key: He had no idea who you were?

Me: No. But seeing his pain was worse.

Key: I thought you had no pity for him.

Me: This man isn't our father anymore. He's something, someone, else. His brain is punishing him.

Key: Why haven't we taken him to a doctor? Why didn't you?

Me: I'm trying to understand what matters.

Key: Dad is sick.

Me: So why not let him be sick here, with us, with the ghost of Mom?

Key: We can't leave him alone in the house anymore.

Me: Let's ask him what we should do.

Key: He's in no position —

Me: But he has opinions.

We called our father down to us, and we sat him at the kitchen table.

Key: Comfortable? Want something to eat? A tuna sandwich?

Dad: I'm fine, thanks. What's going on?

Key (pointing at himself): Do you know who I am?

Dad: You both look familiar, I'll say that.

Key: I'm your son. And so is Rad. We're twins.

Dad (frowning): Where's Diane?

Me: Coming. Give her a minute.

Key: Dad, we're trying to figure out what to do.

Dad: About what?

Key: About you.

Our father looked over at me, then back at Key.

Dad: I'm not sure I understand. What about me?

Me: You're not well. You know that, don't you?

"He's right, John." My mother materialized next to me, across from my father.

Dad: I'm not well. So what?

"They want to know how to take care of you," my mother said. I couldn't be sure if this ghost of my mother belonged to me or to my father or to the both of us. "What's next, John?"

My father sighed and bent his head.

Dad: I want to stay here with your mother.

Me: Shouldn't we take you to a doctor? Shouldn't we see what's going on?

Dad: Why?

Me: What if you get attacked with that headache when you're down in the ravine? You could throw yourself off the platform.

Dad: Yes, that's possible.

Me: That's a problem.

Dad: Is it? Why?

Key and me: ?

Dad: I want to live out my life here. With you and Diane.

Key: Okay, Dad.

Dad: That it? No more questions?

Me: No, Dad.

Dad: I'm going down to sit. The birds, you know? They're back. And the trees with all their baby leaves. The ravine.

My father stood up to go.

"I'll go with him," my mother said. "Even though I hate the ladder."

█

Over the last six months, my father's memory was hit or miss. This made things easier and harder. He seemed calmer, always on his best behavior, polite and gentle, like a guest among strangers. As if he were a lodger without any real connection to anyone or anything around him. Most of the time, though, he kept to himself. He wandered through the house, room to room, muttering, stopping for a few moments as if he'd forgotten where he'd been or where he was going. And he sat down behind the house in his broken chair, looking off across the ravine, looking down, looking inside himself, talking with his dead wife.

The hard part was logistics. Since Key and I agreed not to take our father to a doctor or a hospital unless he needed urgent care, we made sure one of us was always home. We had to know where he was in the house or outside, and we had to make sure he ate, got cleaned up, slept. We kept watches going at night. This meant we traded days at school and figured out weeks when one or the other of us worked more hours at the restaurant. And we agreed to start repairing and renovating the house little by little. Our Plan B, if taking care of our father became too frightening or if we drowned in it, was to sell the house and get him other help. Maybe he would end up dying in a hospital after all.

We didn't really know anything. We were just trying to do our best.

And Key was home alone when our father came at him.

I walked through the front door just as —

"Stop!" I shouted it.

My father held Key against the dining-room wall by the throat, his fist pulled back. Key, bleeding.

I couldn't reach my father before he threw his punch. And my brother crumpled.

I tackled my father, threw him to the floor.

He fought. He writhed and threw out his fists, looking to land whatever punch he could, looking to damage, howling.

Heavier at last, stronger, I clamped my father's wrists against his chest.

I would have killed him. Pure instinct. Pure violence.

"No." My mother at my back. "Rad, no."

I was driving my father's own hands against his throat. His rage turned to deep fear. I'd strangle him with his own hands.

"No, Rad." My brother behind me, his hands on my shoulders. "Please, no."

I'd crush the air out of my father.

"Konrad." My brother, my mother.

My father's face a map of terror.

"Rad, I'm hurt." My mother? My brother? Which?

"I'm hurt. Don't do this. I need you."

And I released my father.

My father, on the floor, curled up, and my mother slapped him. She slapped him hard. "What did you do, John?" My mother, shouting. "What did you do?"

My father hit himself. He hit his head again and again. He would have beaten himself to death, I think, if that were possible.

I did what I could to stop him. I pulled at his arms, and I tried to block his fists. He had new strength.

And then my ghost mother fell on my father.

No, not my mother. My brother. Key climbed onto my father, elbowing me aside, covering him with his body, shielding my father's head from his own fists.

My father was screeching, howling. He was caught under lightning and waves of rain. He was caught by an attacking ocean.

He was a small island, inundated, going under.

My father might have been me. I could see it, see myself. And I felt ashamed. I saw myself in my father, out of control, unable to be consoled or stopped, dangerous.

At last, he collapsed under my brother.

Key had taken more punches. He was badly bruised, bleeding, but alive. He was still holding onto our father.

"Come on," I said. I tried to scoop Key away, but he resisted. "Come on. Leave him be."

Key let me lift him up from the floor, and my father rolled away, covering his face with his hands.

I went to the kitchen for ice, ice for my brother's face, for my father's, and towels.

When I returned, my father was turned against the wall. And Key was lying down behind him, pressed up close, his hand on my father's shoulder.

My brother was love.

NINE

Key and I face each other in the kitchen of our run-down, worn-out house. I've broken a pitcher, pounded a table, punched a refrigerator.

Our father is dead.

We'll have to call the police. I'd wanted to understand what had happened between Key and my father as they stood on the platform. I'd wanted to understand how my father came to fall, but I don't think it matters anymore. Or that it matters beyond the more important truth: that my father is gone, released from himself — and that we, Key and I, are free.

I feel strange. I feel something I may not have felt in a long time, if ever. It feels warm. It feels easy. It feels like control.

Light streams through the windows. My father's ghosts have disappeared. And I'm breathing, steadily, slowly.

I'm at peace.

That's what this is. It's peace.

Jacqui.

I want to call her like I promised. I want to say, "My father's dead." I want to say, "Let's talk."

"You," I want to say. "I really only want you."

I sit back down across from Key.

"I'm sorry for how I've acted," I said. "Sorry for being me. You're my brother, and I —"

"I love you, too."

Silence.

"Key?"

My brother looks at me, drawn and pale, exhausted, his face still swollen, purple from the beating he took two days ago.

"Why did you go down the ladder in the first place?"

"I saw him down there from my room. He was standing right at the edge of the platform. I was scared he would let himself go over. I thought I'd help him back up."

Silence.

"So you went to him, and can you tell me about the dream, Key? What came over you?"

"I'm not sure I can say."

"There will be questions, Key, and I want to understand, if it's possible."

"A dream, when you describe it, always comes out boring or confused. This wouldn't be any different."

"Except Dad dies at the end."

Key looks at me closely. "Something has changed."

"Where?"

"In you."

"I don't know how to describe it."

"Relief," Key says. "I feel it, too, which is why I'm shaking. I'm falling apart from relief."

■

We stood there, Rad. We stood there a long time looking at each other, Dad and I. I had my circular breathing, and I was praying. Have mercy on us, have mercy on us, *over and over. I was talking to any god who would listen. Dad was smiling. I couldn't tell if he could hear*

*me. He said nothing at all. I looked into his eyes. He was
near and far.*

*I could sit here and tell you what I saw if you want
that. I saw his entire life. I watched his parents die of
disease, and his insane uncle go into the hospital again
and again. I watched Dad paint hundreds of paintings,
draw thousands of pictures, and I watched him sketching
out the faces of the people around him, doodling mazes in
his class notes. I watched him sleep and eat and drink and
meet Mom. I watched him take care of her when she was
pregnant with us. I watched him at law school, studying,
arguing, hating every minute, and I watched him pass the
bar. I watched him juggling cleavers, jumping on a bed. I
watched him loving us, loving Mom, and I watched him
lose it all. I watched him punch his client and his boss. I
watched him doubt. He was so afraid. I watched him give
up on us, on Mom. I watched him sleeping with Mom,
always with his hand on her, comforting her, letting her
know he was right there, wouldn't leave, and I watched
him torment her. I watched his whole life come undone.
I watched him lose Mom and bury her. I watched him
grieve. And I watched his mind die.*

*We were standing in clouds and in oceans and in tall
grass. We were standing on the platform he'd made. We
were hugging each other and looking at each other with
a thousand miles between us, a million miles. The whole*

time, I was breathing in and out at the same time, and I heard talking inside myself. A new prayer: Be love.

And then Dad spoke, or tried to speak. I couldn't hear him, Rad. I couldn't hear him because he was standing on, I don't know, an island. An island with strange life. Birds with two sets of wings, giant birds with headdresses and with tails that stretched behind them fifty feet. Wildcats that walked upright and miniature monkeys the size of acorns. And bright flowers with blue teeth. He was standing on an island at the other end of an immense ocean, holding his hands up to his mouth, shouting.

I strained to hear him, but I could only hear myself: Be love.

I reached out across the whole ocean toward his island. I wanted to touch him, Rad. I wanted to tow him in, island and all. I wanted to be love. But he was gone.

█

What had my father done if not let himself fall?

Could this be called a suicide?

Maybe my father thought he was falling backwards into an ocean that would carry him away from his island toward the mainland he had somehow lost.

Or maybe he didn't fall at all. Maybe he dived into his ocean with every intention to swim across all the way home to us.

I don't know. No one will ever know. Key and I can only imagine.

Key cries.

I let him. I don't stop him with my own outburst, my own emotion. I don't stand in the way. I don't interrupt him. I take my brother's hand, and he cries. He cries for everything, everyone. He sobs with relief.

I would watch my mother cry, too, if she were here. If my ghost mother came here to cry for herself, for her husband, for her sons, I would let her. Hasn't she earned the right to be sad? Hasn't she earned the right to wish she were alive?

My mother doesn't come. My mother won't come again.

I watch my brother cry for what seems like a thousand years.

When my brother stops crying, we'll call the police. We will tell them we found our father. We will tell them he's been sick for a long time, and we've been taking care of him. No, we will say, we have no mother. No, we will say, we tried our best. Our father, he was sick, his mind, but we did our best.

The police will shake their heads. They will believe us. And they will go.

Key and I will bury our father. We'll bury him next to our mother.

My brother and I will sell the house and rent an apartment. We'll work. We'll finish our last year of high school.

And when the time comes, my brother will go into his life, and I will go into mine. He will become something remarkable. He will become love while I find my island. We will always be twin islands, close and far at the same time. Maybe I'll end up a monk off the coast of France, or as a hermit on some tiny island in the south Pacific, or as something altogether different. Maybe I'll surprise myself and stay on the mainland, part of the continent. Part of Jacqui.

Right now, though, my brother cries. And as he cries, I'll watch you walk away. I'll watch you keep to the bridge we made. You'll head back to your country, your island. I'll watch your back until you're out of sight.

For MAI and for SM&P

Patrick Downes' first two novels for young adults, *Fell of Dark* and *Ten Miles One Way*, received multiple starred reviews and were named to best-of lists (NYPL Best Books for Teens, Booklist Top 10, Kirkus Best Teen Reads). He is also the author of *Come Home, Angus* (illustrated by Boris Kulikov), a picture book. A New York City native, Patrick divides his time between the United States and Canada.